ULTIMATE SECRETS
Second Edition

by

Lee V. Moore

TELEMACHUS PRESS

Cover designed by Telemachus Press, LLC

Published by Telemachus Press, LLC
7652 Sawmill Road
Suite 304
Dublin, OH 43016
http://www.telemachuspress.com

ISBN: 978-1-945330-83-4 (eBook)
ISBN: 978-1-945330-99-5 (paperback)

FICTION / Thrillers / Espionage

Version 2018.01.12

Table of Contents

ULTIMATE SECRETS

Second Edition

Chapter 1

HE SAT ALONE at a table near the wall in Sophie's Restaurant. For the last twenty minutes, he'd sat anxiously shifting his weight from left to right and occasionally forward, as he awaited the arrival of a man whom he'd never met.

Steven Gregory had requested a table as far from the bar as possible, to assure an acceptable degree of privacy. The modest restaurant was not very crowded, nor was it very noisy, which meant that one could, without much effort, hear almost every word spoken at the adjacent tables.

The early afternoon crowd had come and gone, and only two other tables were now occupied. At the table near the bar sat a large man reading a newspaper; Gregory thought the man had to be at least 355 pounds. His frequent and annoying cough was probably due largely to his chronic cigarette smoking. The man frowned each time he took a drag on his cigarette.

The young couple, sitting at the table off to the left of the large man, had finished eating and was just holding hands now and exchanging smiles. A man at the far end of the bar was sitting alone, and two other men sat near the middle, having a good laugh about a derogatory remark made by one of them belittling a local politician. Gregory glanced at his wrist watch. 2:10 p.m., and there was still no sign of the man whom he had grown to hate immensely, the anonymous caller who had interrupted Gregory's visit with his wife, Freda, who had been hospitalized for nearly twenty-six hours.

The man for whom Gregory now waited was the man who had claimed responsibility for the bomb blast that had caused extensive damage to the daycare center where Gregory's wife worked. She had locked up only a couple of moments after the last child had been picked up by its mother. Freda Gregory had just turned from the front door of the building and started for her car, when suddenly a bomb exploded, sending shattered glass and wood in every direction. Flying debris struck her body violently.

Only a couple of hours before, Gregory had stood over his wife as she lay flat on her back in a hospital bed. He was thankful that she was still alive after having come so close to death. A large white bandage was wrapped completely around her head. Her swollen left cheek was dark blue and resembled the face of a boxer who had taken a terrible beating in the ring. Another bandage covered the small cut on the left side of her neck.

Gregory stared down at his wife, holding her hand affectionately as she slowly regained consciousness, calling his name.

"I'm right here, honey," he said with a frown, as if he could feel the physical pain she was experiencing.

"Steven, what happened?" she asked.

"It's okay, honey," he responded. "Don't worry. It's all right. You're in a hospital."

"Steven?"

"Don't try to talk, honey," he urged. "Just try to get some rest."

"Oh, Steven, it hurts. I'm in so much pain." She was sobbing.

"I'll get someone in here," Gregory said, moving toward the door. As he stepped outside the room into the hall, he looked both ways. Seeing a nurse who was making her rounds, Gregory quickly summoned her. "Nurse, please," he said. "My wife is in a lot of pain. Could you please help her? Something for the pain?" The nurse promptly moved to the room without responding, and Gregory followed.

The room was a semiprivate one with two beds. As he looked on, Gregory leaned backward against the unoccupied bed. The shared phone, positioned midway between the two beds and near the wall, suddenly rang. Startled by the abruptness of the ring, Gregory wondered briefly who could be calling. He hesitated, and then quickly snatched up the receiver.

"Hello," he said.

"We mean business, Gregory," said the heavy voice on the other end of the wire. "It was not a *faulty gas line leak* as reported by the news media."

"What?" said Gregory. "Who is this?"

"Just listen to me! If you don't want your wife to die, you'd better meet with me pronto. The bomb was meant to be a warning. It went off too soon."

Gregory turned suddenly so that his back was to his wife and the nurse. "Who are you?" he growled with a low voice.

"No more questions!"

"Okay," said Gregory. "You have my attention."

"I think you are a smart man, Mr. Gregory. I trust you won't do anything stupid—like going to the police."

"No", said Gregory with a calm voice. "I won't do that."

"Good. And that was too bad about your wife—I mean the bomb and all. But let me assure you, it could have been much worse. The bomb was only a warning."

Gregory closed his eyes as rage and fear rivaled within him. "You said you wanted to talk."

"Meet me at the corner of—"

"No," Gregory interrupted. He wouldn't feel safe meeting the man on a street corner. "I'll meet you at Sophie's Restaurant in one hour. Do you know the place?"

"I know the place," said the man on the other end of the wire. "Be there."

And now, almost two hours later, Steven Gregory sat alone, awaiting the arrival of that anonymous caller. He considered the possibility of a connection between the caller and Fred Ramis, an influential mobster boss from whom Gregory had borrowed money nearly four years earlier. The twenty thousand dollar debt had already been paid in full, after the outrageous interest had pushed the total upward just over one third of the original loan.

Gregory had been anticipating a very promising career as a professional football player. That is, until the accident. Offers from professional ball clubs had been pouring in, with each offer exceeding one million dollars per year. It was during his senior year at college. He had accepted no offers and had signed no contracts. He was only holding out, waiting for the biggest and the best deal.

But then it happened. During a midseason game in the third quarter, after carrying the ball forty yards, he was hit hard, only two yards short of a touchdown. After the dust had settled and the players from the opposing team were peeled from on top of him, Gregory's left leg was broken. And all of those million-dollar offers suddenly went down the drain.

He knew that rehabilitation would be difficult. And with no job, the bills mounted, making Ramis' offers of large sums of money very appealing. Gregory knew that Ramis was a mobster and he was aware of the man's reputation for helping poor souls in need of quick money, and then taking back even more.

Gregory was now doing quite well financially. He was a successful architect, and the owner of his firm. And now he feared what he thought to be inevitable—Ramis now wanted a piece of the action. The pattern was falling into place. It had happened many times in the past, with others. And Gregory was aware of that fact. Ramis would attempt to get a percentage and acquire partial ownership of Gregory's architectural firm, the ex-football player considered, as he sat at the table. Ramis had to be the one behind the bombing of the daycare center. Who else would stoop that low? It was the beginning of his familiar extortionist attempts to make Gregory just another one of his many puppets.

A tall man of medium build entered the restaurant suddenly. His face was clean shaven. The three-piece suit that the man wore was dark. He was well-groomed. Gregory spotted him instantly and wondered if he were the anonymous caller. But the man did not look like a gangster, Gregory considered. At least not one of Ramis' boys. This man looked like a Harvard graduate; a corporate attorney.

The man's eyes focused on Gregory. With a faint smile, he moved slowly to the table and joined him. But before he pulled up a chair and sat opposite Gregory, he paused momentarily, eyeing the ex-football player as if to suggest that he held all of the cards and that this was the end of the road.

"I Trust you didn't have to wait very long for my arrival, Mr. Gregory," said the man who wore the dark suit.

It was him, Gregory thought. He recognized that heavy voice. The man who sat before him was the man who had called Gregory at the hospital.

"You are very prompt, Mr. Gregory," the man added. "I like that."

"Who are you?" Gregory asked seriously, staring at the man.

"Who I am is not important, Mr. Gregory. The important thing is that we respect each other. I represent the people who you now have under your thumb. But let me assure you, Mr. Gregory, we are *very* powerful. And we will not hesitate to employ that power to achieve our goal. When we searched your house a couple of days ago, we didn't find what we were looking for, leaving us no alternative but to confront you directly."

Gregory gritted his teeth but remained silent. He was staring at the man who not only was responsible for his wife being in the hospital but who was also responsible for the break-in and search of his home.

On February 2, two days before, Gregory and his wife had gone out to dinner at their favorite restaurant and then to a surprise anniversary party at a friend's home. It was Gregory's and his wife's tenth wedding anniversary. The dinner and party had been great, but when the couple returned home, shortly after 1:00 AM, they found that their home had been wrecked. At first they thought that they had been robbed, but they later learned that nothing had been taken: no clothing, no jewelry, and no silver. The house had simply been recklessly and unscrupulously searched.

"And what, exactly, are you looking for?" Gregory asked.

"Don't insult my intelligence, Mr. Gregory. You should know now that we are very serious. Just give us what we want and no further harm will come to your wife."

"What does Ramis want?" Gregory asked, growing even more angry and impatient, as he thought of his wife, lying in that hospital bed.

"Who the hell is Ramis?" the man asked.

"He wants to control my firm, doesn't he?" Gregory asked with a slightly louder voice.

"Hold your voice down," the man urged. "We don't want to make a scene here."

"I want you to take a message to Ramis," Gregory continued. "I have paid him back every cent that I've borrowed from him, in addition to outrageous interest."

"What the hell are you talking about?"

Gregory slapped the table violently with his left hand as he removed his right hand from the table. "I will not become another Ramis puppet. I will resist everything he throws at me."

"Don't push me, Gregory. I've told you to keep your voice down."

"You nearly killed my wife, and you tell me to keep my voice down," Gregory growled.

"We want the disk that your Uncle sent to you—*today*. Or your wife will die."

Abruptly, a loud blast was heard.

Steven Gregory sat silently at the table as his rage peaked, and the gun powder filled the air as rapidly as the smell of steak had filled the air earlier. He sat there stunned by the sound of the blast and of what he had done. The man who wore the dark suit, who sat at the table before Gregory, had slid out of his chair to the floor, where he now lay with a bullet in his abdomen.

Gregory had shot the man with the thirty-eight which he'd been holding under the table. He slowly rose from the table and looked at the man on the floor, lying in a pool of blood. Gregory had lost his head. He had only brought the gun along for protection. He had not come looking for vengeance.

The woman who sat with her boyfriend at a nearby table was screaming hysterically, while the men at the bar took a dive to the floor. The very large man who sat at a table alone, reading a newspaper, trembled with fear, with his mouth agape and unable to move a muscle.

Reality suddenly grabbed Gregory with a tight grip. He knew he had to get out of the restaurant very quickly. With the gun pointed downward, by his side, he walked swiftly out of the restaurant to a waiting car at the curb. He opened the door and hopped into the car. The man sitting behind the wheel was Alvin Walker, Gregory's old college pal and close friend.

"Get us out of here, Al," Gregory said urgently.

"What happened in there?" asked Alvin.

"Go! Go, Al! Get us out of here!"

With haste, Alvin pulled into the traffic. When they were about a block away from the restaurant, he said, "I heard a shot back there, Steven. What happened?" Only then did he notice the gun in Gregory's hand. "Where did you get the gun?"

"I shot a man, Al," Gregory said.

"God, Jesus Christ!" Alvin whined. "Why did you do that? What's going on Steven?"

"He tried to kill my wife!" Gregory growled. "He was responsible for the bomb explosion that almost killed Freda!"

"I don't understand what's going on here, Steven," Alvin said with a trembling voice. "You told me to bring you to the restaurant to meet someone. You didn't tell me you wanted to 'kill' someone. I don't like this, Steven. I don't like this at all."

"It's done, damn it! I guess I lost my head."

"Is he dead?"

"I don't know. He's a gangster. He works for Ramis. It's either me or them, Al."

There was a moment of silence as Alvin drove on; then he said, "What do we do now?"

"Just keep driving," Gregory said. "Don't stop."

"Do you think we're being followed?"

"I don't know," Gregory admitted. "I don't think so." He turned and looked through the rear window.

"How did you get involved with Ramis? He's a mobster, man. He's bad news."

"It's a long story, Al. I needed some money some years back. I got a loan from Ramis. The rest is history. You know how he operates. He's a bloodsucking son of a bastard."

There was a pause.

"Well, we can't just drive for the rest of the day. We should go to the police."

"We should and we will," Gregory clarified. "But not until I get my wife out of that hospital."

"She's in bad shape, Steven. She shouldn't be moved."

"She's as good as dead if we don't get her out of there. Ramis plays for keeps." Gregory shifted his stare to Alvin. "Take me to her, Al. Now."

Alvin looked at Gregory and there was silence. He focused his attention on the road once again as he steered the car into the direction of the hospital.

~~~~

It was almost 3:00 PM when they arrived at the hospital. Gregory pushed the car door open hurriedly, with great force, causing it to spring back and bump his leg as he put one foot onto the pavement.

"Wait a minute, Steven," said Alvin, as he watched his closest friend attempt recklessly to get out of the car. "You'd better leave the gun here." Gregory paused for a moment, and then tossed the gun onto the car seat. "Keep the motor running. I won't be long."

They had parked in a no parking zone, directly in front of the main entrance of the hospital. The car would have to be moved, Alvin thought, as he saw a uniformed security man moving toward him, waving a hand, suggesting that he should clear the area.

Gregory had jumped from the car, closing the door with a slam, and had raced toward the sliding doors and was now entering the building. The lobby was almost empty. Only a man, leaning against the wall, and reading a magazine, and a young woman sipping water from a plastic bottle, were present. Straight ahead at a semicircular information desk sat two hospital employees. One was taking a telephone call, and the other was directing an elderly woman to the billing office.

Gregory moved quickly past the desk to the elevator doors. He pressed the button, and the doors opened. Once in the elevator, he pressed the button for the fourth floor. The doors closed. He had ignored the request by the man who was trying to catch a ride up in the same elevator.

As he traveled upward, Gregory thought of the man whom he had shot in the restaurant. It had happened so quickly and so spontaneously. And he now wondered if the man had died there on the floor. "I'm a murderer," he thought. He had never fired a gun at anyone in his life until that day. He closed his eyes and tried to justify his actions. Recalling his wife's bandaged head and the bomb blast which nearly killed her, he found no difficulty justifying his actions.

The elevator doors opened, and he stepped out quickly, on route to Room number 405.

Steven Gregory was a large man with a muscular physique. He seemed to shake the floor with each step he made as he moved down the corridor.

He approached the door to his wife's room, and pushed it open. What he saw caused him to feel very uneasy. He moved slowly toward her bed, but she was not there. The bed had been made up with fresh sheets and bedcovers. Maybe she was in the bathroom, he considered. He called her name and opened the door to the bathroom, but no luck there either. She was gone.

Now he really started to worry. Where could she be? He tried desperately not to panic. There had to be a logical explanation for her absence. Maybe they transferred her to another room. But why would they do that? Did her doctor request more x-rays, perhaps? Maybe she was in the lab for tests or something. But regardless of the reason *why* she wasn't in her room, Gregory had to find her.

He left the room and started down the corridor to the nurses' station. Sitting at the desk was a petite young nurse with short black hair.

Gregory got her attention promptly. "Nurse," he said, with both hands on the desk, "I'm looking for Freda Gregory—my wife. She's not in her room."

"Is she ambulatory, sir?"

"She was in pretty bad shape when I left a couple of hours ago. I'm sure she's not just walking around exploring the hospital. Could you please check to see if maybe her doctor requested that she take some tests are something? X-rays perhaps?"

"What's her room number, sir?"

"Number 405," Gregory pointed. "Freda Gregory."

The nurse picked up her prescription glasses from the desk and looked over the charts and records before her, for a brief moment. Then she said, "Sir, there is no patient by that name assigned to Room 405. In fact, Room 405 hasn't been occupied for the last couple of days."

Gregory stood bewildered and speechless. He could not believe his ears. He swallowed with difficult and said, "You're out of your mind. I left my wife only a few hours ago in that room." He pointed. "Room 405."

"Sir," the nurse said. "Maybe you're on the wrong floor."

"I'm not on the wrong floor!" Gregory growled loudly.

"What's going on here?" said the nurse who had just exited from the supply room. She was the RN in charge of the floor. She was a large, tough-looking woman with short brown hair. "This 'is' a hospital, you know?"

"Where is the nurse who was here a couple of hours ago?" Gregory asked. "She was sitting at this desk. She looked in on my wife." Gregory struck the desk violently. "Damn it. I'm not crazy. I want to know what's going on here."

"I've told you, mister," said the large RN. "This is a hospital and you're out of order. And if you don't leave right now—"

"I'm not leaving without my wife," Gregory said.

The RN looked at the nurse behind the desk and said, "Call security."

Before the nurse could reach the receiver, Gregory snatched the phone violently from the desk, disconnecting the wire. Then from one room to the next, he searched for his wife. When he reached the fourth room from the nurses' station, in the distance, at the end of the long hall, Gregory saw two doctors wheeling a gurney onto an elevator. Atop the gurney was a woman who was hooked up to an IV bottle.

Without thinking, Gregory called Freda's name and charged down the hall to the elevator. As the doors were closing, Gregory forced the doors back open and stormed onto the elevator and shouted, "Where are you taking her?"

The two doctors were startled and speechless. When Gregory moved to the head of the gurney, he saw that the woman on the gurney was not his wife.

For a moment, he just stared at the woman without speaking a word as the elevator doors closed.

"Hey, buddy," said one of the doctors. "What's your problem?"

"Shut up!" Gregory snapped, as he looked malevolently at the man. Then, with the bottom of his fist, he struck the button for the first floor.

The two doctors would not dare speak another word.

When the doors opened on the first floor, Gregory stepped off the elevator quickly and shoved his hands into the pockets of his beige London Fog jacket. With anger in his eyes, he started down the lengthy corridor. Something was wrong. Something was very wrong. His wife had vanished without a trace.

As he walked down the corridor, Gregory could see a security guard in the distance talking into a radio and moving toward him. The security guard stopped suddenly and eyed Gregory with suspicion.

Gregory began to reduce his pace, coming to a complete stop. Why was that security man eyeing him that way, Gregory thought. Perhaps he had been alerted by the head nurse on the fourth floor.

"Hey you," the security man said to Gregory. "Wait!"

Gregory slowly turned in the opposite direction and began walking away. Looking over his shoulder, he noticed that the security man had started to walk faster toward him. With his hands still in the pockets of his jacket, Gregory, too, started to walk faster until he saw the security man running toward him.

Gregory removed his hands from his pockets and began running down the long corridor. He had no idea where the corridor would lead him; he just knew he had to get away.

From one long corridor to the next, the security man chased Gregory until Gregory reached the emergency room area where he stumbled into a gurney on which rested a shrouded corpse. The impact was so great, the gurney overturned and Gregory fell to the floor.

The security guard caught up with him and pulled him up from the floor. As Gregory got back to his feet, he forced the security man back violently against the wall, dazing him; then he struck the man's face with his fist.

An alert intern came to the aid of the security man, grabbing Gregory from behind, almost lifting his feet up from the floor. Gregory quickly stomped the intern's foot, and then gave him an elbow to the chest, sending the man reeling backward. Two more interns became involved, each grabbing an arm and standing on either side of Gregory.

Gregory kicked the man at his left on the knee; and then, with the force of his powerful arm and the sweep of his foot, the ex-football player tripped the man, sending him down to the linoleum floor very hard. The other intern struck Gregory's face with a right hook, but no damage was done. With both hands, Gregory grabbed the man's clothes near the chest area, spinning him around and forced him backward against the wall. He blocked a punch that the intern threw, and then grabbed the intern by the hair; and with both hands, smashed the man's head backward, against the wall, repeatedly, while nearly a dozen individuals, who had come to the hospital emergency room for treatment of broken bones or lacerations, found themselves scrambling away from the sign in desk.

The security man, who had been chasing Gregory, attempted to aid the intern, by grabbing Gregory's neck from behind with his arm. Gregory released the intern's hair and tried to reach backward for the security man's head. Unsuccessful in that attempt to free himself from the man's powerful grip, Gregory reached quickly for the man's groin with a stiff slap, made a fist and pulled upward with a very firm grip. He did not let go until the security man was on his knees crying for mercy. Gregory turned and faced the man, punched him once in the chest, and then with his knee, struck the side of the man's face.

For a brief moment, Gregory stared downward at the incapacitated security guard, and then quickly exited the hospital, running through the emergency room entrance, just as the two large doors sprang open for two ambulance attendants who were wheeling in a victim of an automobile accident which had occurred only a few blocks away.

From the side of the hospital to the front entrance, Gregory ran like there was no tomorrow. In the parking area, after taking a quick look around, Gregory spotted the car that he and Alvin had pulled up in. He ran to the car and fumbled with the car door, then finally snatched it open and hopped in.

"Get us out of here," Gregory exclaimed, breathing deeply. "Quick!"

"What's wrong?" Alvin asked. "What happened?"

Gregory didn't have time to answer questions. With the engine already running, Gregory stomped Alvin's foot which was on the accelerator, and the car took off quickly burning rubber.

"What the hell are you doing?" Alvin shouted, as he and Gregory wrestled with the steering wheel to avoid hitting two young women who were heading to their car in the hospital parking area. The grey Chevy missed the two women just barely, but came even closer to smashing into the side of a blue pickup truck, as Gregory and Alvin dashed from the hospital parking area into the traffic, still wrestling with the wheel.

Only when they were about a block away from the hospital did Gregory settle back and turn the wheel over to Alvin. The exhausted Gregory sighed deeply, closing his eyes as he leaned toward the door opposite Alvin.

Alvin was so excited, he didn't know if he should be angry or frightened. "What the hell was that all about?" he asked with trembling hands, his heart pounding. "I mean what?"

With his face buried in his hands, Gregory sniffed. "They've got her, Alvin. They've got my wife." Gregory sat upright and stared aimlessly through the car window. "They took Freda."

Alvin was stunned. "What do you mean? Who has Freda? She's supposed to be at the hospital."

"She's gone!" Gregory snapped. "They say she was *never* there."

"That's crazy," Alvin said. "We both visited her earlier today."

"I knew Ramis was a powerful man, but I didn't think he had that kind of power. They have no record of my wife's being there. They're lying."

Alvin was silent for a moment. Then he said, "Maybe it's not Ramis that you are dealing with."

"Of course, it's Ramis," Gregory insisted. "He's a powerful bloodsucking mobster. Who else could it be?"

"When you were in the hospital a minute ago, I had the car radio on. A special news bulletin came on. It seems that the man who you shot in the restaurant was not one of Ramis' thugs."

"Then who the hell was he?"

"He was an FBI agent."

There was a moment of silence.

"That's crazy," said Gregory. "The man who I shot was the same man who searched our home and who was responsible for the bomb that nearly killed Freda. The FBI isn't in the terrorist business."

"I'm just telling you what the news report said," Alvin clarified. "And it doesn't look good. Your name was also mentioned, Steven. According to the report, the FBI agent was attempting to make an arrest, when you pulled a gun and shot him. He's still alive."

"But I'm not wanted by the FBI."

"Maybe not last night, but today you are."

"The man at the restaurant was a gangster," Gregory insisted. "And why would the FBI want me anyway?"

"You said yourself that you didn't think that Ramis was powerful enough to make Freda disappear from the hospital without a trace. Think about that, Steven," Alvin urged. "Ramis' power is no greater than a high school principal, compared to the FBI."

"The FBI is not in the kidnapping and extortion racket," Gregory said.

"I know what I heard, Steven," Alvin said. "It was no mistake. The man who you shot in the restaurant was an FBI agent."

Gregory was silent for a moment and suddenly recalled the words of the man in the restaurant, only seconds before he shot him: "We want the disk that your uncle sent to you—today. Or your wife will die."

"Oh, My God," said Gregory, now realizing that what Alvin was trying to convey to him could indeed be true. "That guy may have really been an FBI agent. He mentioned something to me about a disk that my uncle sent to me."

"Your Uncle Max retired from the FBI last year, didn't he?" asked Alvin.

"Yes," said Gregory. "But I haven't received any damned disk from him or anyone else. All I know is that my wife has disappeared without a trace, and it seems that somehow the FBI is involved."

As they drove on, Gregory started to feel physically awful. He thought he might vomit as he considered his options. He didn't know whom to trust. He could not go to the police, for they too were looking for him, in conjunction with the FBI, for the attempted murder of a Federal agent, whom he felt was responsible for the bomb explosion which had nearly killed his wife.

There was only one man, he thought, who could shed some light on the subject of his problem; and that man was Gregory's Uncle Max, who up until the previous year was the Director of the FBI. Gregory knew without a doubt, that it was absolutely imperative that he contact his uncle very soon if he wanted to see his wife again.

Chapter 2

IT WAS NEARLY 4:00 PM when Gregory and Alvin pulled over to the side of the street and parked near the curb. Just ahead, about six houses down, Gregory saw a dark car parked near the curb, one house down from Alvin's house.

"Why did you want me to pull over?" asked Alvin.

"Look up ahead there," said Gregory. "You see that black car parked in front of your neighbor's house?"

"Yeah," said Alvin.

"It's a government car," Gregory said.

"How do you know that?"

"There are two men sitting in that car, and I'll bet all of my chips they're not there to collect your neighbor's rent. They are FBI agents and they're on to you. Those bastards are probably watching everyone that I am in contact with—friends and family. How long will your wife be out of town?"

"Brenda won't be back for another week," said Alvin. "She's visiting her mother in New York."

"Good," said Gregory. "Turn around and get us out of here."

Alvin hesitated for a moment, staring at the rear of the dark car which was parked, in the distance, near the curb. "Maybe it's not the FBI," he offered.

"We can't take that chance," said Gregory, as he watched Alvin's face.

He knew that his old college buddy had begun to worry and debate tacitly if he had gotten too involved with him. Alvin was a loyal friend, but he was not the toughest of men. He would snap under pressure and Gregory realized that fact.

Alvin finally turned the car around and they left the neighborhood.

Gregory knew now that no place would really be safe. He'd thought that he could hide at Alvin's house for a while, re-examine his situation, and contact his Uncle Max, who would hopefully have some answers. Alvin's house was now off limits, so Gregory would now have to take his chances at some pay phone. But not until after dark. The police and the FBI were combing the city. He didn't want to increase his chances of getting caught, as a result of being spotted on the street.

At dusk, the grey Chevy pulled over to the curb on Clayborn Street. It was nearly sixty degrees out, when Gregory opened the car door. "Circle the block," he said as he stepped out of the car. "Twice, if you have to." He closed the door, and then stepped backward from the Chevy as Alvin pulled off.

Gregory turned toward the sidewalk and shoved his hands into the pockets of his jacket. He was almost certain that the FBI, by now, had as much information on Alvin as they had on himself, including a detailed description of Alvin's car and license plate. Gregory didn't want to take the chance of having a police squad car cruise by and spot the Chevy, while he was standing in the phone booth only a few steps away.

As Gregory moved to the phone booth at the corner, he noticed that the street was not very crowded. In fact, it was almost deserted. Most of the traffic was on Royal Street which ran through Clayborn at the intersection.

He entered the phone booth quickly and closed the door behind him.

The smell of cigarette smoke was heavy, left behind by a previous occupant. Gregory reached into his left front trouser pocket, pulled out a quarter, and inserted it into the appropriate coin slot. It was a long distance call to Washington, D.C. He gave the operator the number and she rang his uncle's home.

"Steven, my boy," said Gregory's uncle, on the other end of the wire. "I thought your business was doing very well." He chuckled. "It has been quite some time since you've called *collect*."

"Uncle Max," Gregory said quickly. "I'm in trouble!"

"What kind of trouble?" His voice grew serious.

"I shot a man."

"Good Lord, Steven," said Max, detecting the urgency in Gregory's voice. It was no joke.

"I don't know his latest condition."

"But why did you do it?"

"They tried to kill Freda. They have my wife, Uncle Max. They took her from the hospital."

"They? They who?"

"The FBI."

"Wait a minute, Steven," said Max. "Slow down. You've lost me."

"The man who I shot was an FBI agent."

"Are you sure?"

"I'm pretty sure."

"Where's Freda?"

"They took her from the hospital, Uncle Max. I don't know if she's dead or alive."

"I can't believe this has happened. Where are you, Steven?"

"I'm in a phone booth at the corner of Royal and Clayborn."

"Give me that number."

"I can't stay here, Uncle Max. They're all over the place."

"Listen to me, Steven. I still have some contacts within the bureau. I need to make a call and I'll call you right back."

Gregory hesitated before giving his uncle the phone number, then said, "I don't know if I can stay."

"Trust me, Steven," said Max. "You'll hear from me within five minutes."

The dial tone.

Gregory could hear only the dial tone. He removed the receiver from his ear and hung up with a slam.

One minute elapsed, then two, then three. Then Gregory saw Alvin pull up to the curb and stop. Gregory signaled with his hand for Alvin to circle the block once more and he did.

From the opposite side of the phone booth, a man stood tapping the glass with his knuckles, trying to get Gregory's attention. The man pointed to his wrist watch. "You've been in there for a while, buddy," he said. "I need to use the phone."

Gregory was surprised by the man's abruptness. Because of his incoherence, he could see that the man had been drinking. The man started to push against the door, attempting to enter the phone booth.

Gregory opened the door. "I'll just be a minute longer, pal," he said. "Just take it easy."

"I need to use the phone, now!" The man's eyes were open widely, bulging maniacally. "Either you come out of their or I'll pull you the hell out!"

"There's no need to get upset," Gregory said. "I'm waiting for a very important call."

"Hell with the call," the man said as he grabbed Gregory's jacket at the collar. "You're coming out of there, now." Gregory was about to push the man away when suddenly a car pulled up and stopped near the curb about nine yards from the phone booth. It was a solid black car with all of the windows rolled down. While staring briefly at the car, Gregory found himself being forced backward against the rear of the phone booth by the angry man who had wanted to use the phone.

Gregory had been forced backward, just in time to miss the bullet fired from a forty-four, which caught the man in the head. The single shot had come from the direction of the car which had just pulled up. Only seconds after the first shot was fired, two other men from the same car opened fire with automatic weapons, spraying the phone booth. Within ten seconds, it was all over. The shooting stopped and the car sped off.

When Alvin completed the circle around the block, he once again approached the curb and the phone booth. As he viewed the bullet-riddled telephone booth, he felt as though his heart had dropped to his stomach.

"Oh, God, Jesus Christ!" he shouted hysterically. He didn't know if he should check on Gregory or just keep going. It had all happened only seconds before he had pulled up.

He quickly looked all around him as he sat in the car in shock. He wondered if the gunmen were still near as he noticed a few pedestrians cautiously looking on from a distance.

"Oh, God, help me," Alvin said, then hopped out of the car, forcing his numb body to move toward the phone booth. The smell of gun powder was faint, but still detectable. Blood was visible on portions of shattered glass which was just barely hanging from the frame of the booth.

Blocking the entrance of the phone booth was the corpse of the impatient man, who had attempted to force Gregory out of the booth. Underneath the dead body lay Steven Gregory, as motionless as a corpse, with a blood-soaked shirt, near his chest area.

"Oh, God, no," said Alvin as he grabbed the dead man by the shoulders and pulled him off Gregory who lay flat on his back. "Steven," Alvin called as he knelt over Gregory. "Steven! Please don't be dead."

Gregory suddenly opened his eyes. "I'm not dead," he said. "Help me up."

"Oh, God," said Alvin. "Thank God!"

Miraculously, Gregory had not been hit. The blood on his chest came from the fragments of the dead man's brain which had oozed from the large hole in his head. After being shielded from the bullets by the dead man's body, Gregory had kept his body very still and pretended to be dead.

But now Gregory was racing Alvin to the waiting grey Chevy. Once in the car, they sped off, leaving the area quickly.

"Damn it!" said Gregory. He leaned backward against the seat, holding his head back and looking aimlessly upward at the darkness, in the direction of the top of the car. "That was just 'too' close back there."

"Thank God you were not hit," Alvin added with a trembling voice.

For the next few minutes, they drove without speaking a word. They were both trying, but with little success, to get over the shock of Gregory's close call with death.

Then suddenly, Gregory broke the silence.

"Uncle Max was going to call me back," he said. "He's probably the only person who can help me now. I've got to get to a phone."

"Why don't we just leave town," Alvin suggested. "I don't want to go near another phone booth."

"I can't leave without knowing something about my wife."

"We might as well face it, Steven," Alvin began with regret, glancing at Gregory and then the road, and then to Gregory. "She's probably dead already."

"Don't say that," said Gregory.

"You saw what they just tried to do to you."

"Don't say that!" Gregory shouted, grabbing Alvin's shoulder tightly. He shoved him aggressively, causing him to momentarily lose control of the car. "She's got to be alive."

When Alvin regained control of the car, there was once again silence. They were drained both mentally and physically.

"Okay," said Gregory. "Whoever it is who was trying to kill me, probably thinks that I'm dead, after that phone booth episode. So maybe we are just a bit safer now."

"But when they find out that you're not dead, all hell will break loose again."

"So we'll be careful," said Gregory. "Take me to Eddie's Strip Joint. We're not far from there."

"Why do you want to go there?"

"I need to contact Uncle Max. I can use the phone there. I know the owner."

"Aren't you afraid someone might recognize you?"

"The place is a strip joint. All eyes will be focused on the naked women on stage. I'll feel safer there. I don't think that the people who are after me will try anything in the presence of so many people. Besides, they think I'm dead."

~~~~

Eddie's Strip Joint was both fuliginous and vociferous. The cigarette smoke was thick, Gregory thought, as he entered the show area. A very healthy-looking woman with shoulder length brown hair and large breasts, and wearing only a yellow bikini, was dancing to the beat of a popular Kool & the Gang tune, while the crowd urged her to *take it all off!*

Gregory slowly moved through the crowd, heading for the bar. He had zipped his jacket completely to hide the blood stains on his shirt.

"You'd better take the gun this time," Alvin had said, as Gregory started to get out of the car, in the parking area on the left side of the strip joint. "And zip your jacket," Alvin added. "The blood stains."

Gregory sat at the bar for at least a half minute before he saw the owner of the strip joint, Eddie Masterson, who had introduced Gregory to the mobster Fred Ramis many years ago when Gregory was having money problems. As usual, Eddie was dressed very well, wearing a black pinstripe, three-piece suit. The collar of his silky pink shirt was open widely, exposing the thin gold chain around his neck. He was a well-groomed man with a clean-shaven face. A lengthy scar, a reminder of his early days of violence, was visible on the left side of his face from his ear lobe to his chin.

When Eddie spotted Gregory sitting at the bar, he broke off his conversation with one of his dance girls and stared blankly at Gregory, as if he were surprised to see him. After Signaling with his head for Gregory to join him in his office, Eddie led off and Gregory followed.

The office was a room to the right of the bar. Standing just outside the door was a mountain of a man, a guard with his arms folded. He stood about seven-two, with no hair on his head. Mean face. Gregory thought the man had to be at least three hundred pounds of muscle.

Eddie entered the office first and Gregory followed, closing the door behind him.

"The streets are just a bit dangerous for you these days, don't you think?" said Eddie. "I never thought I'd see the day that you'd be in the drug business."

"What are you talking about?" asked Gregory, surprised.

"It's all over town," Eddie said. "The FBI is on to you and your cocaine connection with Ramis."

"That's a lie, Eddie," Gregory insisted.

"Yeah, I know that," Eddie admitted. "But that's the word on the streets: the FBI was attempting to make a drug related arrest when you shot the agent in the restaurant—that's the word on the streets. They're really trying to fuck you good, Greg baby. But the question is why?"

"I have no idea," Gregory said, as he moved toward Eddie's desk and sat on the edge of it. He'd begun to feel warmer in the office. He unzipped his jacket. His blood-stained shirt was visible.

"Gee shit, Greg," Eddie said eyeing Gregory's shirt. "You need a doctor."

Gregory raised a hand. "No, it's not my blood."

"Well, what happened?"

"Someone is trying to kill me. All signs are pointing toward the FBI, but I don't know why. At first I thought it was your boss."

"Ramis wouldn't do that," Eddie said. "You've paid back your loan in full, plus interest. Besides, Ramis knows that you and I are pretty close. He wouldn't do anything to hurt you because of the obvious consequences. And by the way, Ramis is now my ex-boss. I now have new and more powerful connections with Chicago and New York. Ramis is on his way out."

There was a knock at the door.

Gregory jumped up from the edge of the desk quickly, pulled his gun, and pointed it in the direction of the door.

"Take it easy, Greg baby," said Eddie, staring at Gregory. Then he looked at the door. "What is it?"

"You have a visitor, boss," said the heavy voice on the other side of the door. "Godfrey is here. Do you want me to send him away?"

"No, Rocco," said Eddie. "I'll be right there." He looked at Gregory. "It's okay, Greg."

Gregory lowered the gun. "I need to use your phone."

"On the desk," Eddie pointed. "Look, I've got to take care of a little business outside. Whatever you want, it's yours." He left the office.

Gregory moved to the phone on the desk and grabbed the receiver. He phoned his Uncle Max in Washington once again, but this time he dialed direct without the assistance of an operator.

"Uncle Max?"

"Steven!" Max shouted. "I—I thought that something had happened to you. I called you back, but the line was dead. I thought you had perhaps given me the wrong number."

"Someone took a couple of hundred shots at me while I was waiting for your call. The phone booth was sprayed with automatic fire."

"My God, are you okay?"

"Just barely, Uncle Max. What did you find out?"

"The bureau has been infiltrated."

"What do you mean?" Gregory asked with a frown. "I don't understand."

"It has something to do with a big case that I was investigating before my retirement, last year."

"But what does that have to do with me?"

"It has nothing to do with you—other than the fact that you are family."

"And what exactly was this big case that you were investigating?"

There was a pause, and then Max said, "The FBI is not what it used to be. Things have changed within the system."

"What things?"

"There is an internal struggle going on. And that's all that I can tell you right now. I want you to come to Washington. I can protect you here."

"I can't do that, Uncle Max," Gregory insisted. "It's too dangerous. The FBI is everywhere."

"But listen to me, Steven. You've just told me that they tried to kill you moments ago. Now, there's a good chance that they think you're dead. I want you to go to the Airport. Your ticket will be waiting for you at United's ticket desk under the name of Tom

Greenwood. I've made arrangements for you to fly here to Washington immediately."

"But Uncle Max," said Gregory. "What about my wife? She's—"

"You're plane leaves at 7:58 PM San Francisco time," Max interrupted. "For God's sake, Steven, be on that plane. You can't help your wife if you're dead."

The dial tone.

Gregory could hear only the dial tone. His uncle had hung up. "Uncle Max!" Gregory shouted. Then he put the receiver down with a slam.

~~~~

San Francisco's International Airport was busy when Steven Gregory arrived. It was seven thirty-six P.M. when he entered the main terminal building. He had paused briefly at the electric eye controlled sliding doors, recalling his uncle's instructions. As he moved promptly toward the ticket desk, the doors closed behind him.

There was no line at the United Airlines ticket desk. Gregory had no problem getting his plane ticket. Everything was in order. The female ticket agent gave him his one way ticket to Washington, DC with a smile.

"Have a nice flight, sir," she said.

Gregory nodded and smiled faintly. He turned from the desk with a new sense of confidence. His Uncle Max had come through for him.

"Flight 87," announced a female voice over the loudspeaker system, "now boarding at Gate 7."

Gregory suddenly looked at his ticket and learned that he would be departing on United's Flight 57 at 7:58 PM, just as his Uncle Max had told him. But Flight 57 is the number that caused him to suddenly feel uneasy. He had noticed that same flight on the board on the wall behind the ticket agent. On the blackboard was a list of flight arrival and departure times spelled out with white numbers and letters.

Gregory turned and started toward the ticket desk again, for a better view of the board. He learned that flight 57 would not be departing on time.

"Excuse me," Gregory said to the ticket agent. "Is this an accurate update?" He pointed to the board on the wall. "I mean, about the departure delay of Flight 57."

"Yes, sir," she confided. "I'm afraid there will be a twenty-minute delay." Gregory sighed, and then moved away from the ticket desk. Now it would be almost forty-five minutes before his plane would leave and that made him feel very uneasy. Under normal circumstances, the delay would not be a problem. But Gregory had become paranoid, and he didn't know who was watching him or who might be the next to take a shot at him.

Gregory would be boarding the plane at Gate 5, so Gate 5 is where he would now go. He followed the signs and the arrows as he walked down the lengthy corridor, and he thought of his wife. A sick feeling came over him once again. He had no way of knowing if she were dead or alive.

But then suddenly, his attention was drawn to the Airport Security man just ahead, who was speaking into a radio. Gregory made a dash for the men's room and wondered if the security man had spotted him. He paused at the door for a moment, and then opened the door slightly, just enough to look down the corridor. The security man was gone.

Gregory closed his eyes and sighed. He remained in the men's room a while longer, then left. When he reached Gate 5, he would not sit in the chairs provided. Rather, he moved to one of six telephone units near the wall and slid the door shut. He sat down and picked up the receiver. He was now alone and it was quiet. He turned his face away from the door as much as he could in an attempt to prevent anyone from recognizing him.

He didn't have any more change in his pockets, so he pretended to put a coin into the coin slot and dialed seven numbers at random, just in case someone was watching him. For nearly fifteen minutes, he kept the telephone receiver to his ear and periodically pretended to be talking to someone on the other end of the wire, whenever someone would approach as if to want to use the phone.

But suddenly, Gregory noticed a man in the distance staring at him. When Gregory's eyes met his, the man quickly shifted his gaze away from Gregory, but did not move.

Gregory slowly faced the phone and hung up the receiver. He looked back in the direction of the man who had been staring at him, but the man had vanished. Gregory slid the door open, and then stood.

"Flight 57," the voice on the loudspeaker said, "now boarding for Washington, DC, at Gate 5."

Once again, Gregory noticed the man who had been staring at him, but this time the man was not alone. He stood with two other men. All were wearing dark suits.

Something was going on, Gregory thought. He attempted to get in line to board his plane when suddenly a large man with a mustache stepped in front of him and presented his ID.

"FBI," he said. "Let's not make a scene, Mr. Gregory; I'm not alone. Please, come with me."

Gregory felt thoroughly defeated at that moment. He had come so close to making the flight. And he was desperate. The coat of the FBI agent who stood before him was open, and Gregory could see a portion of the man's gun. Without considering the consequences, he reached for the man's gun, but without success. The agent grabbed Gregory's wrist and a struggle began.

Gregory pushed the man backward against a group of individuals who were about to get in line to board the plane. Then suddenly four other FBI agents drew their guns and moved in.

"FBI!" shouted one of the agents. "Freeze Gregory!"

All of the would-be passengers at Gate 57 dropped to the floor. The agent's voice competed forcefully with the screams of panic. "Don't move!" The agent shouted.

Gregory stood very still with his hands raised high.

The agents moved in quickly. One searched Gregory's body while the others held their guns on him. Then Gregory was handcuffed and was led away from the area. As they walked quickly with Gregory, an agent was on either side of him, each holding him by an arm, to prevent him from attempting to run away.

Gregory had no idea what was going to happen to him. The agents would not respond at all to any of his questions.

"Where are you taking me?" he asked as they continued to move quickly to exit the terminal building. "I want to know what's going on." Then Gregory spoke a bit louder. "What have you done with my wife? Where is she?"

Once they reached the outside of the main terminal building, the silence was finally broken. The man whom Gregory had first noticed watching him, while pretending to talk on the phone, said,

"Just take it easy, Mr. Gregory. We have our orders. All of your questions will soon be answered."

The agents had parked directly in front of the entrance of the main terminal building. Their two black cars were parked near the curb in a no parking zone.

Gregory was helped into the back seat of the first car while an agent sat on either side of him. Two agents got into the second car, while the fifth agent got behind the wheel of the first car and looked over his shoulder at Gregory.

"Take the cuffs off," the driver said to the agent, sitting at the right of Gregory. "I don't think Mr. Gregory will give us any trouble."

Gregory remained silent as the cuffs were removed. There was nothing that he could do. An armed agent sat on either side of him. He felt very sure that he'd never see the sun rise again. His uncle had stated that an internal struggle for power was currently going on within the FBI and that many things had changed within the system. But what did all of that mean?

Bright lights suddenly blinded everyone in the car. The agent behind the wheel attempted to shield his eyes by raising a hand. "What the hell," he said, frowning. A car had pulled up quickly and had almost skidded into the front of the first car in which Gregory was held.

A man got out of the car with haste and fumbled with a gun. Gregory recognized the man. It was Alvin. He fired once into the windshield of the first government car, hitting the driver in the arm. Gregory took advantage of the situation quickly by striking the face of the man at his left, who was already sitting close to the door. The impact of the strike was so great; it pushed the man's head against the window and cracked the glass.

The man at Gregory's right was reaching for his gun, when Gregory turned on him and grabbed his neck and his hand simultaneously. Gregory struggled unsuccessfully to take the gun from the agent, then finally released the man's neck and gave him an elbow to the face. He pushed the door open and shoved the agent out, after getting his gun.

Gregory jumped out of the car and fired three times into the windshield of the second government car, as the two agents in that car lowered their heads. Then he rushed to the grey Chevy, opened the door and hopped in.

The car sped off backward, with Alvin behind the wheel. It stopped suddenly, the front wheels turned quickly and then the car sped off forward into the opposite direction, into the lighted darkness, and left the airport.

~~~~

In front of the main Airport terminal building, the blue and red lights atop four police cars, which were parked adjacent to the two government cars with the shattered windshields, revolved brightly. The FBI agent who had been wounded in the arm was being lifted into an ambulance on a stretcher.

Another government car had pulled up behind one of the police cars on the scene. And after receiving a detailed report from one of the agents who was present during the actual shooting, Special Agent Crumwell was on his way back to his car to contact, and convey the facts, to his superiors.

Crumwell opened the door of his car, sat behind the wheel and grabbed the telephone receiver. He contacted his superior, Inspector Miller.

"Sir," said Crumwell, "I have bad news. Steven Gregory has escaped."

"What the hell happened, Crumwell?"

"They had him, sir. But he got away. He had some help, sir. A car came from out of nowhere; a guy jumped out and started shooting."

"Damn it, Crumwell," said the inspector. "Do you know what this means? Do you know what's at stake?"

"I understand, sir. The local police are cooperating fully. We have every available man working on the case—priority one, sir. We 'will' find Gregory."

"Soon, Crumwell; you'd better find him very soon."

The dial tone.

Miller had hung up with a slam.

Crumwell sighed and paused for a moment, holding the receiver to his ear as he stared forward.

Chapter 3

A CAR TRAVELLED at a high rate of speed on a lonely, dark road. It was the grey Chevy. Gregory and Alvin had been on the road just over an hour now, and the incident which had occurred at the Airport was still fresh in their minds.

Alvin had been so shaken up by his role in freeing Gregory at the Airport, that when the two were about four miles away, Alvin had to pull the car over to the side of the road and let Gregory drive.

"I thought you had already left the Airport," Gregory said. "Thank God you hadn't. You pulled up just in time, pal."

Alvin was still a little shaky. "I—I parked the car, then I started to come into the terminal building, just to make sure that you'd get off okay. But then these two black cars pulled up. One guy got out of the car and flashed his ID at the Airport Security guard and then asked if he'd seen you. His partner was showing the security man a picture of you. You'd had about a fifteen minute head start on them. When they entered the building, I panicked. I didn't know what to do. I thought they might gun you down right there at the Airport."

Alvin was nervously rubbing his forehead as he leaned against the car door. He sat upright suddenly, trying to regain his composure. "I didn't know who to turn to. So I waited for a while. I don't know how long. Soon I saw them bring you toward the exit. I rushed to get my car, and then everything happened so quickly." He looked at Gregory. "Do you think I killed the driver of that first car?"

"I don't know," Gregory answered. He glanced at Alvin and saw him rubbing his face with both hands. He was a nervous wreck. Gregory soon reduced the speed of the car to reduce his chances of being stopped by a police officer for speeding. As an occasional car with bright headlights approached him on the opposite side of the road, he thought of his wife. And then he thought of his Uncle Max.

~~~~

On the morning of February 2, Steven Gregory was awakened by the gentle nibbling at his ear by his wife. "Happy tenth anniversary, sweetheart," she said.

Gregory's eyes were only half open when she gave him a big wet kiss on the lips. She had already gargled, he thought. Her breath was minty fresh. Then he opened his eyes widely and said, "Happy anniversary to you too, baby." He sighed, and then jokingly added, "Oh God, has it really been ten years? Feels like it's been twenty-five."

"I beg your pardon," she said, pretending to be angry.

"Well, let's face it, woman. You have been hell to live with."

"Steven Gregory—you liar." She pinched his thigh twice and each time he giggled.

"Okay," he said finally, grabbing her hand. "I'm sorry. Damn—if you didn't pinch two chunks of meat from my leg."

"It serves you right."

"I was only joking, honey," he said with a smile. "It's been ten beautiful years." Gregory pulled her closer and they kissed.

The doorbell chimed suddenly.

"Who the hell could that be?" said Gregory.

His wife sighed, sat upright on the bed, and then tied her robe.

"Maybe they'll go away," said Gregory.

"I'll see who it is, honey," she said.

Gregory tried to prevent her from leaving by gripping her hand tighter.

"I'll only be a minute," she smiled.

They were staring at each other. Gregory released her hand after the doorbell chimed again. "Sixty seconds and counting," he said.

She left the bedroom and went downstairs. When she returned to the bedroom, she was carrying a package with her.

"It was a delivery man, honey," she said

"Who's the package from?"

"It's from your Uncle Max." She hopped onto the bed and gave him the package. "Quick—open it up. Let's see what's inside."

Gregory opened the package and inside he found a bottle of wine, with a note attached to it. He read the note aloud:

To Steven and Freda on their tenth wedding anniversary. Hi kids. I hope to see you within a week when I start my vacation. We can celebrate together.

Love and hugs,

Uncle Max

"He remembered," said Gregory. "Good old Uncle Max."

"He's so sweet," Freda said.

"And do you remember—ten years ago today—Uncle Max sent us a bottle of champagne because he couldn't be at our wedding. Remembered that?"

"Of course I do," she said. There was a brief pause. Then she added, "I have an idea. Let's wait and open it when Uncle Max gets here. He will be here within a week. He's always loved great wine. We can celebrate together."

"Sounds good to me," said Gregory.

"You really love him, don't you?"

"Uncle Max is the greatest," Gregory said. "He married my mother's sister about twenty-five years ago. I remember it well. I was about five years old at the time. It was the first wedding I'd ever intended. It was beautiful. But then my parents died shortly after that. It was an automobile accident. Afterwards, Uncle Max was like a father to me. He took me in and raised me. He took me fishing every chance he could; a little camping."

"Sounds like you had great fun together," said Freda.

"We sure did." There was a pause, and then Gregory continued. "Aunt Angie died twelve years ago. Uncle Max never remarried."

"Oh, why not?"

"I don't know. But you'll have plenty of time to ask him that question and many more when he arrives in a few days."

~~~~

It was nine thirty-eight PM when the grey Chevy pulled over into an old ill-kept gas station just off the lonely dark road.

"Why are we stopping here?" Alvin asked. "Are you crazy?"

"We're almost out of gas," Gregory answered calmly. "A car with an empty gas tank is no good to us."

The gas station attendant had started slowly toward the car.

"Damn it, Steven," Alvin said. "What if that guy recognizes you?"

"He probably won't."

"Can't take that chance," Alvin said, as he opened the car door. "Don't let him see your face. Look away from him." He got out of the car with haste and met the gas station attendant. "Hi, pal," he said. "We're in a hurry. Would you fill her up for me, please?"

"Yes sir," said the attendant. "Regular or unleaded?"

Alvin did not hear the man. He was nervously looking all about, wondering if a police car would pull up at any moment.

"Hey, buddy?" The attendant persisted.

"What?" said Alvin.

"Which type do you want?"

"Oh, ah—unleaded. Please."

The young attendant hopped over to the gas pump and started to fill the tank of the Chevy.

Gregory sat silently behind the wheel looking into the rearview mirror at the gas station attendant. Gregory thought he might be in his mid-twenties. His hair was long and looked dirty.

Gregory lifted his blood-stained shirt away from his chest for a brief moment, and then let it go. The smell was sickening and the shirt felt very uncomfortable against his skin. He could hear Alvin and the gas station attendant talking, but he could not make out what was being said. Alvin glanced at the road suddenly and Gregory could hear the nozzle being pulled from the opening of the tank. It was done. The tank was now filled to capacity.

Alvin paid the gas station attendant and got back into the car.

The gas station attendant stood and watched as the grey Chevy pulled off. Then he went back inside and moved to the telephone beside the cash register. He grabbed the receiver and dialed seven numbers. As he waited for someone to answer on the other end, he pulled up an adjacent wooden chair with rungs and sat down.

"Hello," the attendant said, finally. "Let me speak to Deputy Perkins."

There was a pause

"Yeah, Sam, this is Jack," said the gas station attendant. "You know that grey Chevy that you told me to be on the watch for?"

"Yeah," said the voice on the other end of the wire.

"Well, it just pulled out of my gas station, heading east. Same license plate and everything."

"Good boy, Jack. That's going to make those Federal boys very happy. I'll contact them now."

Chapter 4

FBI INSPECTOR, ANTHONY Miller, sat behind his desk in his office awaiting the arrival of a man whom he had employed in the past to take care of his dirty work.

Miller was a man with a heavy build and a pot belly. He was now in his early fifties, a veteran agent with the FBI. He had recently learned of Steven Gregory's bold escape from the agents at the Airport, and he knew that something had to be done quickly, for Gregory was now a very "high risk"—that was the word from his superiors.

Steven Gregory's file had been pulled and was atop Miller's desk. Miller had thumbed through the thick file earlier viewing the photos of Gregory and his wife and the other typed information on both of them—their background, before and after their marriage to each other.

He was about to grab up a cigar from the box on his desk and have a smoke, but there was a knock at the door. "Come in," he said.

The door opened slowly and a tall slim man entered the office and closed the door behind him. He stood about five-eleven, perhaps one hundred and sixty pounds. His face was as usual, expressionless and clean shaven. The hair on his head was neatly trimmed. He was well groomed.

His name was Carl Hilderbrant, a professional killer. With a cold and insensitive face, Hilderbrant stared into Miller's eyes, as he moved slowly toward him and sat in the chair in front of Miller's desk.

"I'm glad you could come on such short notice," Miller said. "This one is 'really' important."

"They are all 'really' important, Mr. Miller," Hilderbrant said. "Just give me the facts."

"Steven Gregory is the focus," Miller began. "Here is his file." He pushed the folder to Hilderbrant. "Gregory must be exterminated immediately." Miller grabbed up the briefcase from the floor beside his desk and then placed it on top of the desk.

Hilderbrant raised a hand in response to the briefcase being placed on the desk. He knew it contained a large sum of money. It was standard procedure. "I didn't say that I'd take the job yet."

Hilderbrant looked at a five-by-eight photo of Steven Gregory, and he read some typed information before him. He learned that Gregory was six feet and one inch tall; his weight was two hundred and nineteen pounds; his hair was black; his complexion was dark; his eyes were brown. Hilderbrant looked at the photo again, stared at Gregory's strong face and admitted tacitly that Gregory looked like a tough man.

Then Hilderbrant's attention was once again drawn to the typed information before him. He read that Gregory was an ex-football player, and that he was currently a successful architect and the owner of his firm.

"There's twenty thousand dollars in this briefcase," Miller said. "You get twenty thousand more after the job."

Hilderbrant shifted his gaze from the information on the desk and stared at Miller's eyes. "The largest amount you've ever paid me to do a job was ten thousand—flat. Now you offer me four times that amount. So, tell me, Mr. Miller. What did this man do to deserve so much attention?"

"As in the past, Hilderbrant," Miller clarified, "Your job is to exterminate—period. The reason for extermination should not concern you."

"Why don't you just give the word to your field agents to kill Gregory On site?"

"No flattery intended, but my superiors feel that you are the 'best' in the business. They wish to employ your services for extra assurance."

Miller didn't like Hilderbrant and that was no secret. The feelings that the two men had for each other were mutual.

"What was Gregory's last location?" Asked Hilderbrant.

"He was apprehended at the Airport a short while ago, but he escaped. As of now, Steven Gregory could be just about anywhere. In the file their," Miller pointed. "You'll find some names and addresses of individuals whom he might contact for help. He has some friends in the underworld and will probably seek help from them first."

"Or he may try to make a run for it on his own," Hilderbrant offered.

"Well, this much is for certain—he's currently being assisted by a longtime friend named Alvin Walker. He's the one who helped Gregory escape from the Airport. Now, should you decide to take the job, you will be working in conjunction with Special Agent Crumwell. He's a good man."

"Won't work, Miller," said Hilderbrant. "You know I work alone, and without rules or restrictions."

There was a moment of silence as Miller stared at Hilderbrant. "As you wish," the FBI inspector said finally. "Does that mean you'll take the job?"

Hilderbrant grabbed the briefcase from the desk, opened it, and looked at the money inside. Then he looked at Miller, and in response to the question, he said, "It means that we will do business."

Miller just stared silently at the man whom he considered to be nothing more than a cold-blooded killing machine.

~~~~

It was almost eleven-thirty PM when Carl Hilderbrant arrived at Eddie's Strip Joint. Hilderbrant had learned of Eddie's acquaintance with Gregory from the FBI file which he'd studied at Miller's Office. Hilderbrant had an amazing photographic memory and he now knew as much about Steven Gregory and his acquaintances as did the FBI.

Eddie Masterson was the first name on Hilderbrant's list, and he was aware of Eddie's connection with powerful mobsters; so Hilderbrant reasoned that Gregory might seek help from his old high school buddy, Eddie, and perhaps ask him to help him hide out for a while from the FBI.

Hilderbrant sat at the bar for nearly twenty minutes before Eddie approached him. Hilderbrant had spoken to the bartender and had asked to see Eddie.

"I'm Eddie Masterson. What can I do for you?"

"Your friend, Steven Gregory, is in big trouble," said Hilderbrant. "I'd like to help him. But in order to do that, I need to know where he is. And I was hoping that you could help me."

"Who are you?" Eddie asked.

"A mutual friend," said Hilderbrant. "Can you tell me where he is?"

"We're not in touch," said Eddie. "I haven't seen Gregory in years."

"Did you know that the FBI was looking for him?" said Hilderbrant. "He shot one of them earlier today."

"I wasn't aware of that," Eddie lied.

"Don't play games with me, Eddie," Hilderbrant said, leaning forward.

"The FBI has set Steven up for a big fall. You and I both know that Steven is not in the drug business with Fred Ramis, but the FBI is trying to prove that he is."

There was a pause. Then Hilderbrant continued, "I can help, Eddie. If you are half the friend that Steven told me you are, let me help."

Eddie was buying Hilderbrant's story, but he didn't want him to know that just yet. He wanted to test him further, so he invited him back to his office to try to find out more about him.

Hilderbrant rose slowly from the bar and followed Eddie. By referring to Gregory by his first name and by pretending to be a friend and by talking against the FBI, Hilderbrant had started to win Eddie's confidence.

Standing just outside the office door was Eddie's king-sized, baldheaded bodyguard, with his arms folded.

"Rocco," said Eddie, "I don't want to be interrupted."

The large bodyguard nodded and watched as Eddie and Hilderbrant entered the office. Then he closed the door.

Eddie started toward his desk and said, "Okay, *Mr. Mutual Friend*. Why don't we start by you telling me who you really are and what's your relationship with Gregory?"

Eddie was about to sit on the edge of his desk when he turned and faced Hilderbrant. He found himself staring into the barrel of a handgun with a silencer.

"Don't do anything foolish," said Hilderbrant, with his usual calm voice. "I want you to move slowly behind that desk and sit down; keep your hands where I can see them."

Eddie complied with Hilderbrant's request. "Who are you, man? What do you want with me?"

"Don't talk," said Hilderbrant.

Eddie's hands were raised high as he sat in the chair behind the desk. He was really frightened, but he didn't want Hilderbrant to know that. "If you want money, I can get it from the safe. It's yours, baby." He was smiling faintly.

"Put your hands down on top of the desk," said Hilderbrant.

"Anything you say," Eddie complied.

Hilderbrant pulled up a chair and sat in front of Eddie, facing him. "Now I want you to take your time and call Rocco in from the door the way you would normally call him. And remember," Hilderbrant added, "I'm watching your face. So, no signals, or you become a dead man. Understand?"

"No problem."

"Once Rocco is in here, I want you to have him close the door behind him. Call him now."

"Hey, Rocco!" Eddie said. "Come in here for a minute."

The door opened and the big man looked inside and said, "Yeah."

"Come in for a minute," said Eddie, "and close the door."

Rocco entered and closed the door.

Hilderbrant was sitting so that his gun could not be seen by Rocco. As the large bodyguard moved toward the desk, Hilderbrant concentrated on the sound of each heavy footstep the large man made, until he felt that he had the exact location of his target.

Without turning around to take aim, Hilderbrant placed his gun upside down on his right shoulder and fired three bullets in the direction of the heavy footsteps. Rocco fell to the floor a corpse.

Before Eddie could reach into his desk drawer for his gun, Hilderbrant gave the chamber of his gun a spin and pointed it at Eddie.

"Don't try it," said Hilderbrant.

Eddie quickly raised his hands high. "Don't shoot."

"Move backward away from the desk," said Hilderbrant.

Eddie slowly pushed himself away from the desk as he sat in his swivel chair with rollers.

"There's one bullet left in the chamber of this gun. Only 'I' know where the bullet is. Every time I get the wrong answer to my question, I'll pull the trigger."

"I'll tell you anything you want to know," said Eddie. "Just ask."

Hilderbrant was a master at inducing fear. He had killed Eddie's bodyguard only to establish his lack of respect for human life. The bodyguard was no more than a pawn in Hilderbrant's game of chess.

"Where is Steven Gregory?"

"I don't know," Eddie answered.

Hilderbrant squeezed the trigger. But the gun did not fire.

"Where is Gregory?" He asked again.

"God, I swear, I don't know where he is."

Hilderbrant pulled the trigger and once more, the gun did not fire.

"He was here earlier!" Eddie shouted with fear. "We talked a little, and then he left. That's all, I swear, man. Don't kill me."

"What did you talk about?"

"He told me that the FBI was trying to kill him, but he didn't know why. He used the phone, and then he left."

"Who did he call?"

"I don't know. I swear, I don't know. I left my office at the time. I don't know who he talked to and I don't know where he is now. What more do you want from me?"

Hilderbrant stared at Eddie briefly, and then answered. "Nothing more." He pulled the trigger and the gun fired. The bullet jerked Eddie's head back and he fell from the swivel chair, dead.

Hilderbrant calmly rose from the chair, removed the silencer from the gun and returned the gun to the holster on his left side, under his dark jacket. The silencer was slipped into his coat pocket as he turned and looked at the dead bodyguard on the floor.

He left the office swiftly and closed the door. The music was loud when he reached the main show area. The dance girl with long brown hair was almost completely nude as she worked the stage to a tune made popular by the Rolling Stones. There was clapping and cheering as many smoked and drank.

Hilderbrant shoved his hands into the pockets of his jacket. Without looking back with even a trace of remorse, the unconscionable killer left the building, thinking only of Steven Gregory.

Chapter 5

"I THINK I'M going to be sick," said Alvin Walker as he and Steven Gregory traveled down that lonely dark road.

"Are you sure?" Gregory asked. "You mean like vomit?"

"I mean, like yeah, man—the works. Stop the car. Stop the car, now."

The car was moving at the rate of 65 miles per hour. Gregory approached a curve and started to reduce the speed of the car quickly, but the car did not stop until they were just out of the curve.

Alvin quickly opened the door and got out of the car.

Gregory kept the engine running and kept the headlights on. He could hear Alvin but he could not see him. Darkness was all around them.

Ahead was an S-shaped curve. Halfway through the curve, in the distance, Gregory saw bright blue and red lights flashing rapidly in the darkness. It looked as though a terrible automobile accident had occurred. About six police cars seemed to be blocking the road.

A car suddenly pulled around the parked grey Chevy and headed toward the police cars ahead. Gregory watched as the car stopped about one tenth of a mile ahead. A policeman with a flashlight stepped out in front of the car and directed the driver to stop. A man got out of the car and two policemen shined their flashlights into the front and back seats of the car. Then Gregory saw the driver of the car move to the back of the car as the trunk was opened and searched by the policemen.

It was a roadblock, Gregory concluded. There was no automobile accident. He looked at the open door opposite him and called Alvin's name. "Hurry up," he added. "We've got to get out of here."

Alvin did not respond. Gregory got out of the car in haste and almost got himself killed. An eighteen wheeler had just come out of the curve behind them, moving a bit faster than it should have. The driver of the large truck blew his horn and locked the wheels when he saw Gregory.

Gregory was blinded by the lights but jumped out of the way of the large truck just in time. The smell of burnt rubber was in the air. After the driver was sure that Gregory had not been hit, he roared the engine of the eighteen wheeler and started forwarded toward the roadblock, leaving a string of obscenities in the air behind him.

At the roadblock, a policeman ordered the truck driver to stop, and then he approached the truck. "What the hell were you skidding for?" The officer said. "Can't you handle that thing?"

"There was a stupid sonofabitch and his car in the middle of the road back there," said the truck driver. "He stepped in front of me."

"Is that a fact?" said the officer.

"I think I'll check it out," said the second officer. He moved to his car and hopped in.

Gregory had just returned to the grey Chevy and sat behind the wheel, after helping Alvin into the car. Gregory was about to put the car in reverse when suddenly the police car with bright flashing lights, pulled up in front of them and stopped. The cars were face to face, and almost bumper to bumper.

"Oh, God," said Alvin. "Will this night never end?" He was holding his forehead, frustrated.

Gregory just sat still for a moment with his hands gripping the steering wheel very tightly. When he saw the policeman get out of the police car, he slowly turned the power steering wheel counterclockwise as far as it could go. He shifted the car to reverse, and then stomped the accelerator. The car spun backward and almost lined up evenly with the police car. It was now on the right side of the road, facing the same direction as the police car.

The police officer quickly shielded himself behind his car and drew his gun, as Gregory fired two shots into the right front tire of the police car and sped off into the darkness.

The police officer at the roadblock just ahead, who was checking the truck driver's ID, surprised by the two gunshots, rushed to his car radio and heard the voice of a policeman say. "It's the grey Chevy. They just shot out one of my tires. I repeat, it's the grey Chevy. Gregory is getting away. I need assistance."

The roadblock broke up and all of the remaining five police cars sped off in pursuit of the grey Chevy.

"Oh, God," said Alvin. "We're going to die. If they catch us, we're dead."

"Not if I can help it," said Gregory. "You just hold on."

For nearly fifteen minutes, the chase continued. Gregory and Alvin drove past the same gas station where they had earlier purchased gasoline. About thirty seconds behind them were the five police cars with sirens blasting and blue and red lights flashing.

The gas station attendant watched with excitement as the cars roared along the road in front of him.

By now, police reinforcements had been contacted by radio. And still another roadblock was being formed, nearly three miles down the road, ahead of Gregory and Alvin.

~~~~

Special Agent Martin Crumwell had been awakened shortly after 1:00 AM by the ringing telephone in his apartment. He had stretched out on the sofa in the living room, hoping to get at least a couple hours of sleep. He had been assured by the local police that he would be notified promptly if there were any leads as to the whereabouts of Steven Gregory.

He had contacted his superior, Inspector Miller, and conveyed the news of Gregory's bold escape from the FBI agents. Then Crumwell left the Airport and went to his apartment. He had decided to leave the search in the hands of the field agents and local police, concluding that there was nothing more he could do until morning. But he'd left strict instructions that he was to be notified if there were any contact with Gregory.

The telephone rang twice before he answered it. Crumwell learned that contact had been made with the grey late model Chevy. He learned that the Chevy, while trying to avoid a roadblock, ran off the road.

When Crumwell arrived on the scene, the police officer in charge filled in the details.

"They were traveling at a very high rate of speed," the officer said. "Apparently, when they realized that the road was blocked, they made a quick turn and ran off the road. Before escaping into the woods, they fired at us and we returned fire. But I'm sure that one of them was hit. There are bloodstains on the front seat of the car."

"Did you hit Gregory?" Crumwell asked.

"We don't know," the officer answered. "And, of course, it is dark."

Crumwell suddenly moved with the officer to the grey Chevy on the side of the road. The tires had dug into the soft shoulder, deeply imbedding them in dirt and uprooted weeds. The car had spun around completely so that the front of the car was now facing the road. A blast from a policeman's shotgun had shattered the windshield.

As the policeman pointed his flashlight inside the car, Crumwell saw the blood stains on the seat.

Crumwell stood upright and looked toward the darkness of the forest.

"They could be just about anywhere," he said. "Okay, I want every available man you've got. We're going in at dawn. We don't have to worry about them going very far tonight."

~~~~

Shortly before four A.M., Gregory and Alvin lay amid thick damp weeds and tall trees. It was still very dark and though they could hear each other, they could not see each other. Alvin had been shot in the right shoulder before getting out of the car. Gregory had already fired twice at the first police car which had stopped.

Gregory had put an arm around Alvin's waist and they both scrambled in the darkness, bumping against tall trees and wild scrubs which tripped and scratched their bodies. After running continually for nearly fifteen minutes in the darkness, they suddenly stopped and lay exhausted and very still. They listened to determine if they were being followed.

"I don't hear anyone following us," said Gregory. "We can rest here."

"Why do you suppose they didn't come in after us?" Alvin asked.

"Maybe it's because we have a slight edge," Gregory said, breathing deeply. "They know that we are armed. And if they come after us, shining their flashlights, we could pick them off easily. I think we're safe until morning."

At daybreak, Gregory moved over to Alvin and tried to help him to his feet. "Time to move out, pal," he said.

Alvin frowned. "No, I can't go on," he said. "You'll have to go on without me."

"I won't leave without you. We're in this thing together. I'll carry you if I have to."

"Use your head, Steven," said Alvin. "It's you who they want. I'm bleeding. I've lost a lot of blood. I'm too weak to move. I'll only slow you down." Alvin's voice was getting weaker.

Gregory had been helping Alvin to sit up, but then he lowered him back down to the ground, allowing him to lie stretched out horizontally, with his eyes closed.

Gregory heard the sound of dogs barking in the distance. Full sunrise was perhaps five minutes away. He looked down at Alvin one last time and stared at the body which lay as motionless as a corpse. He called Alvin's name but there was no response. Gregory was about to check Alvin's pulse when suddenly the sound of dogs barking became even closer.

Gregory rose to his feet quickly, starring at Alvin's motionless body. He's dead, Gregory concluded. He must have bled to death as a result of that large shoulder wound. His friend had lost a great deal of blood during the night.

The sound of dogs barking.

Gregory pulled himself together and moved quickly away from the sound of barking dogs. As he ran, he kept his hands extended forward to shield his face. But occasionally a twig would slip through his defenses, slapping him in the face and leaving many painful scratches and bruises. His football training was never like this.

He suddenly tripped and fell flat on his face. He was tired and his lungs ached, but he could not stop. He picked himself up and began running again.

Nearly fifty state and local police were on Gregory's trail. They were armed with shotguns and handguns. Numerous tracking dogs were leading the search. Special FBI Agent Crumwell also assisted in the search. There was so much at stake. He wanted to get to Gregory perhaps more than anyone else, for he was in charge of the operation and he needed results. His superiors were counting on him to get the job done.

Gregory approached an open area. He was finally out of the woods, but not out of danger. He was now even more vulnerable. There were fewer trees to hide behind. He now had hills and slopes to deal with. And he thanked God that his body was in good shape. He was a health nut and that was a good thing. He would normally run two miles almost every day before going to work. He had been well-disciplined from his athletic training.

But even a man with his stamina would have to break pretty soon, considering his previous day which had been both physically and mentally draining. And on top of that, he'd had no sleep during the night.

Gregory finally came to a dead end. There was only one way to go and that way was up. He had come to a steep hill which seemed impossible to climb. The only alternative was to turn in the opposite direction and face the dogs, the police, and the FBI. He dropped to his knees and found it difficult not to admit defeat. He was just too tired to climb that hill.

It was becoming even lighter now. The morning was chilly, but Gregory had not noticed. He had already worked up a big sweat. He was exhausted. But suddenly, high above him, just over the steep hill, the horn of a car sounded off loudly. The car lights were still on. It must be a road, Gregory reasoned. Perhaps the driver was blowing for some animal which had run out in front of his car. Gregory had heard a car's tires screeching to a halt.

But the fact remained—there *was* a road just over that steep hill and Gregory felt that it was his last chance to avoid being captured and or killed. He could perhaps hitch a ride to safety or stop a car by force. It was at least a possibility and he had no other choice. He had to take that chance. Alvin was dead, he concluded, and now they were after him. It was now or never. He got back to his feet with a new surge of optimism. With all of his might, he tackled the hill, gripping shrubs and pulling his body upward until he was over halfway up.

And then it happened. Gregory's foot slipped on a rock and his body started to roll down to the bottom of the hill. He rolled over on his back, frustrated, and struck the ground with the bottom of his fist. His lungs felt as though they would burst. His chest was burning and he was so exhausted.

The sound of the barking dogs was getting very close now. Gregory forced himself back to his feet and started climbing the hill once more. He just had to make it this time. There was no time to lose.

This time he moved slowly and carefully, not recklessly and frantically like the first try. When he was within one yard of the top of the hill, he heard a dog barking at the bottom. The dog was a distance ahead of the pack, but that was just a bit too close for Gregory. He tried desperately to reach the top, but he slipped. Then he gripped deeply into the soil and roots of a patch of weeds and slowly and carefully pulled himself up, inch by inch, until he reached the top, where for a couple of seconds he laid breathing deeply, trying to catch his breath.

Suddenly he felt something pulling at his leg. Gregory panicked. The tracking dog had climbed the hill after him and was biting his leg. Gregory rolled over on his back, pulled out the gun which he had stuffed tightly under his waistband and shot the dog once, killing it.

He got to his feet and started to run down the paved road. He knew the police had heard the shot and would increase their pace. So he too increased his pace. He considered crossing over to the other side of the road and trying for the woods again, but he decided not to, reasoning that the dogs would tear him apart within minutes.

Suddenly, up ahead, Gregory saw a very large truck heading toward him, traveling at a rapid rate of speed. He didn't know if he could stop the truck, but he had to give it a try. He started waving both hands over his head trying to get the driver's attention. It worked. He was standing in the middle of the road, in front of the eighteen-wheeler, when it finally came to a smooth stop. He had momentarily shoved the gun behind him under his pants.

Gregory quickly moved around to the driver's side of the truck and pointed the gun at the driver. "Raise your hands high," he said, "or I'll blow your head away."

"Anything you say, buddy," said the driver.

Then Gregory moved to the other side of the truck, never taking the aim of the gun off the driver, pointing it to the windshield. He opened the door, climbed into the truck and slammed the door shut, keeping the gun pointed at the driver. "Now drive," he said.

The driver complied with the request. He accelerated slowly and the truck took off smoothly.

As the truck passed by the area where he had shot the dog, Gregory saw two more tracking dogs sniffing at the dead dog and the immediate area.

"Just drive," said Gregory, "and keep both hands on the wheel."

"You're the boss," said the driver calmly. "I won't give you any trouble."

Gregory had made it. It had been a narrow escape for sure, but he had made it.

"And where are you headed?" asked the driver.

"I don't know," said Gregory.

"You're running from the police?"

"I'm trying to stay alive," said Gregory. "That's all."

As they drove on, it became even lighter. The sun was shining even brighter now. And Gregory got a better look at the driver. He was a large man. No muscle, just fat. His hair was long and black. He wore a thick beard and mustache. He reminded Gregory of a big lumberjack. He was wearing a red and black plaid shirt, blue jeans and brown cowboy boots. The man could use a bath. Gregory admitted to himself that he too could use a good hot bath.

After nearly an hour of holding the gun on the driver, glancing periodically at the road and then back at the man at the wheel, Gregory's eyelids became terribly heavy and he found it difficult to hold his head up. He wanted to sleep so badly. He started to tremble slightly. A good hot meal would also be in order.

The truck suddenly hit a bump in the road and Gregory's eyes opened widely. He jumped to attention. And he was in control again. "You got any food in this truck?" He asked.

The driver glanced at Gregory, and then directed his attention to the road again. "In back," he said. "Behind you. There's a sandwich in that brown bag."

Gregory turned slightly and looked at the sleeping area behind the seat. Beside a small pillow was the brown bag. He grabbed it and opened it. Inside was a ham sandwich wrapped in clear plastic. Gregory pulled the sandwich out of the bag and removed the plastic.

While keeping his eyes focused on the driver, he took a bite from the sandwich. It was cold but it was better than nothing at all. He discovered a thermos bottle nearby, filled with coffee. He sipped at the coffee and it was terrible. He frowned.

Almost thirty minutes later, Gregory was once again, about to lose the battle against sleep. The truck driver had been watching him periodically, and was aware of Gregory's difficulty, trying to keep his eyes open while holding the gun up and pointed at him.

Gregory suddenly bowed his head lower than he had ever before. His eyes were completely closed. The truck driver was tempted to make a move to overpower Gregory and take the gun away from him. The driver slowly removed his right hand from the steering wheel and placed it on the seat. He started to inch closer and closer to Gregory's hand which held the gun, now pointed downward at the seat.

Suddenly the driver made his move. He reached for the gun, but grabbed Gregory's hand instead. He had overreached and Gregory reacted quickly.

Gregory tightened his grip on the gun and opened his eyes widely.

At first, he thought he was dreaming. But he quickly realized he was not when the front left side of the truck scraped the side of a car approaching them on the opposite side of the road.

The truck driver had removed both of his hands from the wheel and was trying to take the gun from Gregory, who swung wildly at the truck driver and struck the driver's face. Then Gregory, with that same free hand, tried to steer the truck back to the right side of the road as the truck driver continued to keep a firm grip on Gregory's hand. Gregory dropped the gun between his feet and kicked it toward the door away from the driver. He punched the man in the side repeatedly until the driver was out of breath.

Gregory regained control of the truck and then quickly reached down for the gun and pointed it at the driver's head. "Now here, damn it!" Gregory shouted. "Take the wheel!" He grabbed the man's shoulder. "Take it now!"

The driver was breathing deeply when he took the wheel again.

"If you try that again," Gregory said, breathing deeply, "I'll kill you." He slowly leaned backward against the door opposite the driver, pointing the gun at him.

A car with two state troopers approaching the truck on the opposite side of the road came to an abrupt halt. Then it turned around in the middle of the road and sped off after Gregory and the truck driver. The state troopers had seen the truck moving recklessly from one side of the road to the other.

Gregory heard the siren blasting. Then through the side view mirror, he saw the state troopers coming up rapidly behind them.

"Damn it!" said Gregory.

The truck driver had also noticed the state troopers. "They want me to pull over," he said.

Gregory thought for a moment then said. "Okay, so we'll pull over. Start reducing your speed."

The driver complied.

"Listen to me very carefully," said Gregory. "When you stop the truck, I want you to wait until the cop gets within two yards of your door. Don't give him the chance to ask you to step outside. I want you to then open the door and get out of the truck, but don't move away from the door and don't close the door. I want to see you at all times. Do you understand?"

"I understand," said the driver, as he pulled over to the side of the road and stopped.

"I want you to be very polite. And don't look suspicious. And most of all, remember—I'll be watching you. One wrong move, you are a dead man. Don't make me prove myself to you. I will kill you if you do anything foolish."

The state trooper who was driving got out of the car and moved toward the front of the truck, while the other one remained in the car, talking on the radio.

"Is he out of the car yet?" Gregory asked the truck driver.

"He's over halfway past the trailer."

"Alright then," said Gregory. "Get ready. And remember, no funny stuff."

The driver glanced malevolently at Gregory, and then he opened the door and stepped out of the truck. He remained in full view of Gregory, just as requested.

"Good morning, officer," said the truck driver with a smile. "What can I do for you?"

"Let me see your driver's license, please. And remove it from your wallet, please."

"Sure thing, officer," said the truck driver, reaching for his wallet.

"You were driving kind of recklessly back there. You could hurt somebody driving like that."

"Oh, yeah," said the truck driver, "I can explain that." He smiled as he gave the trooper his driver's license. "I did a very stupid thing. It seems I let 'sleep' get the best of me for a minute there. I had been driving all night, you see. And I was just about to let my partner here take over." He pointed at Gregory and then his eyes focused on the gun barrel which was pointed at him.

"Well, I'm going to have to write you out a ticket. You've got to learn to change drivers before you get sleepy. The road is serious business."

Gregory sat very quietly as the state trooper lectured the truck driver and wrote the ticket. But as he sat there watching the truck driver, Gregory was unaware that the other state trooper was slowly walking toward the front of the truck, with his revolver drawn and on the ready. If Gregory had looked through the side view mirror, he would have seen the state trooper inching his way forward on the right side of the truck.

The second state trooper had not had enough time to tell his partner what he was trying to do. He'd decided to surprise the occupants of the truck in an attempt to lessen the possibility of guns being fired. He slowly walked toward the front of the truck until he got within six feet of the door. From that point, he got much more than he had bargained for.

Steven Gregory's photograph had been widely distributed; and the state trooper recognized his face in the side view mirror. His face was angled just right. He had turned it just enough when he saw the first trooper move to the area near the left front tire where the truck had recently scraped the side of a car.

There was no doubt in the mind of the second trooper that the man he was looking at was Steven Gregory.

On the other side of the truck, the first trooper was looking at the scratches on the left side of the truck.

"Looks like you've already run into something not too long ago."

The truck was red, but some of the paint from the car that the truck had scraped was visible amid the scratches.

"This looks like fresh scratches," the first state trooper said. "Looks like you hit something that was blue."

"Don't move!" Shouted the second state trooper on the other side of the truck, with his gun pointed at Gregory.

Gregory froze.

The truck driver quickly reached under his seat on the floor, pulled out a thirty-eight revolver and shot the first state trooper in the chest. Then he hopped into the truck and slammed the door shut.

Gregory lowered his head quickly below the window. The second trooper fired at him, shattering the window. Before the truck driver pulled off, the trooper had emptied his gun at the truck, while the driver returned the fire twice over Gregory's head at the trooper.

When the large truck pulled off, the second trooper rushed over to his partner lying on the ground. He was dead. The trooper ran back to the car and got on the radio.

The truck driver had placed his gun on the seat and was concentrating on the road. Gregory was stunned that the truck driver had a gun tucked away under his seat, and was unaware that he was, once again, pointing his gun at the driver.

The truck driver looked at Gregory sternly and said, "You can put that gun away, buddy. It looks like we're on the same team, now. And it's about time you knew that this isn't my truck. I stole it from a guy back in Texas just before I killed him."

Gregory lowered his gun and stared silently at the man.

~~~~

Inspector Anthony Miller of the FBI sat impatiently behind his desk awaiting an important phone call on the status of Steven Gregory. He was expecting to hear from Special Agent Crumwell within the hour.

The phone on Miller's desk rang and the inspector snatched up the receiver quickly. "Hello," he said, "Miller here."

It was not agent Crumwell.

"This is Washington, D.C., calling," said the masculine voice on the other end of the wire. "Maxwell Craven has been terminated."

"Well done," said Miller. "Have you learned anything more about the disk?"

"Negative. Craven insisted to the end that his nephew, Steven Gregory, has possession of the disk. He stuck to his original claim about sending Gregory the disk several months ago. Six months ago to be exact."

"So," said Miller, "that means that Gregory knows everything. He must be exterminated immediately. He has the power to bring us all down to our knees and destroy everything that we've worked for. Our lives are at stake, Comrade."

"And now, the question is: Did Gregory talk to anyone about the disk?"

"We've been keeping constant surveillance on his close friends and relatives. They will all eventually fade out of existence. But Gregory is priority one."

"It is now in your hands, Comrade," said the voice on the other end of the wire. Then he hung up.

About eight minutes later, Miller received a phone call from Special Agent Crumwell with news of Steven Gregory's most recent location.

"Gregory has been spotted, sir," said agent Crumwell. "It seems that he hitched a ride with a guy who was driving a stolen truck. It was pure damn luck. The state troopers spotted them driving recklessly. After pulling them over, a routine check was done and they learned that the truck had been stolen. Thanks to the alert trooper, he recognized Gregory just before the truck driver killed his partner."

"I want air surveillance," said Miller.

"It's done, sir," said Crumwell. "We have three helicopters in the sky. We 'will' find him, sir."

"And Crumwell."

"Yes, inspector?"

"We no longer need Gregory alive. Remember that. He must be terminated at any cost. I cannot stress that point too much."

"I understand sir."

~~~~

The large truck traveled at the rate of 75 miles per hour through the interstate traffic. Gregory stared through the windshield at the road, as he sat silently, holding his gun with the barrel pointed downward.

"Well, what are you running from?" asked the truck driver.

Gregory shifted his stare to the driver, then back to the road, and said "I'm running from the FBI." He spoke dryly.

"Why are they after you?"

Gregory hesitated, and then said, "I don't know."

The truck driver giggled. "Don't shit me, man. You mean the FBI is after you and you don't know why?" He laughed. "Or is it just so bad that you just don't want to tell me. Was it murder? I mean what can be worse than murder? You can tell me. Did you rob a bank or something?"

"I'm on the level," Gregory insisted dryly. "I don't know why they are after me."

There was a moment of silence.

Then the driver said, "Sure, pal. Whatever you say."

Gregory thought of his wife briefly and remembered the man who had sat before him at the table in Sophie's Restaurant. The man had claimed responsibility for the bomb blast which had hospitalized his wife. And Gregory recalled his words: "we want the disk that your uncle sent to you."

Gregory had no idea what the man was talking about. His Uncle Max had said nothing about any disk and even more important, his uncle had not sent him a disk. Someone was making a terrible mistake, Gregory thought. And that mistake had caused his rather peaceful life to crumble very rapidly. And what about that disk, he thought. The contents would have to be very important to generate the attention and the concern of so many. His uncle had told him on the phone about an internal struggle within the system. Perhaps the disk had something to do with that internal struggle. It was all so confusing.

Gregory sighed, and then he saw the helicopter flying low over them. The helicopter swooped down from out of nowhere and zoomed in front of the truck.

"God damn—that sonofabitch is flyin' kind of low, isn't he?"

"I think we've got trouble," said Gregory. "That's not just 'any' crazy sonofabitch flying low. It's either the police or FBI air surveillance."

"If he tries to land that thing in front of me, I'll ram his ass."

"He won't have to do that," said Gregory. "An army of state troopers has been given our exact location. Don't forget, you shot a fellow trooper a few miles back. They're coming after us. So here is where I get off. Stop the truck."

"You're crazy," said the truck driver. "There's no way I'm going to stop now. They'll have to kill me. I'm stopping for no one."

"The truck has been spotted," said Gregory. "They know what they're looking for. I'll have a better chance on foot." Gregory pointed his gun at the driver's head, then quickly grabbed up the driver's gun from the seat. "Here is where we part company," said Gregory.

The truck driver looked at Gregory and into the gun barrel pointed at him. Then he stared at the road and gritted his teeth. He stomped the accelerator and the speed of the truck steadily climbed until it reached 90 miles per hour.

"Go ahead and shoot me," said the driver. "Go ahead and splatter my brains all over the seats. You kill me, you'll die too. I'm doing 90 right now. Shoot me, big man; we will both die."

Gregory sat very still, staring at the man. He was at a loss for words.

From the FBI helicopter in the sky, the large truck could be seen pulling out from the pack of cars and other trucks on that interstate highway.

Gregory once again felt that defeat was very near. He knew that it was only a matter of time before a swarm of state police would become visible and start firing at the truck. Roadblocks were perhaps being set up during that very moment, he considered.

Gregory warned the driver once more. "Pull over and stop the truck," he said. "I only want you to let me off. Then you can go on your way."

"You'll have to kill me, hot shot."

"Stop the truck, damn it!" Gregory shouted.

The driver tried to increase the speed of the truck even more, but suddenly, with a desperate move, Gregory struck the truck driver's temple with the butt of the gun. And the driver slumped in the seat.

Gregory grabbed the wheel and tried to keep the truck under control, but he was unsuccessful. The large truck had been in the right lane, but suddenly switched over to the left lane as Gregory reached for the brakes. He ran two cars off the road in the process. When he finally found the brakes, he stomped the pedal, locking the wheels and the massive truck started skidding in the middle of the road.

Gregory had lost control of the truck but tried to regain control as he crashed into the side of another car, running it off the road.

More cars ran off the road, trying to avoid crashing; and a terrible chain reaction occurred. One car after another slammed into each other. From the FBI helicopter in the sky, the pile-up resembled a demolition derby. Cars were crashing and overturning rapidly, until the total reached eighteen.

When Gregory finally stopped the truck, he sighed. The truck driver was out cold, with a trickle of blood visible on the side of his head. Gregory pushed away from the driver and hopped out of the truck. With one gun tucked under his waistband and with the other in his hand, Gregory moved to the rear of the truck and was shocked at what he saw.

The interstate traffic had stopped and two lines of automobiles had started to form. Some cars had run off the road and had overturned. The immediate area was a maze of wrecked cars and confusion. Some passengers of wrecked cars, who were not seriously injured, were attempting to get out of their cars; and some individuals who were not involved in the accident tried to help those who were trapped or pinned inside overturned cars. Holding his gun down-

ward by his side, Gregory looked up at the FBI surveillance helicopter circling the area.

Some impatient individuals began cautiously driving through
the maze of wrecked cars. In the distance, Gregory could see about
four state trooper cars with flashing lights, coming up quickly on
the bumpy and grassy side of the road and making their way to the
accident area.

Gregory knew he didn't have much time. He had to leave the
area fast. He didn't want to force his way into someone's car, but
under the circumstances, he had no alternative. And he felt badly
about that. He felt like a wanted criminal. A true John Dillinger.
But in fact, he was only a victim of circumstances.

Gregory hopped into a nearby black sports car which was occupied by only one man. The driver had come to a full stop due to
the traffic jam. Gregory pointed the gun at him and said, "Please.
Don't panic. I don't want to hurt you. I just want you to get me out
of here. Understand?"

The driver of the black sports car froze and swallowed with
difficulty. "Yes, sir," he answered, "I understand."

The black sports car pulled off slowly just as the first state
trooper car reached the accident area.

Gregory looked through the rear window of the car and sighed
deeply as the accident area gradually disappeared into the distance
behind him.

"I want to get off the interstate highway," Gregory said. "Turn
at the next exit."

The young driver of the car looked at Gregory and said, "What?"

"I said—" Gregory realized that he was competing with the
car radio and turned the volume down. "I said I want you to get off
the interstate highway. Turn at the next exit."

"Yes sir," the young man said.

He seemed to be in his early twenties, Gregory thought. He looked like a college student. His hair was dark and cut short. He was thin with a narrow face.

"Where are we going?" The young man asked.

"I'll let you know when we get there," said Gregory. "You have nothing to worry about."

"Are you going to kill me?"

"Of course not," Gregory said. "I only need transportation. Here—" He placed the gun that he was holding in his hand, between his feet. "Does that make you feel better?" He raised both hands for a clear view. "I don't want to hurt you; I don't want your money. I'm just a man who's trying to stay alive. Please. Believe me."

~~~~

Almost forty minutes after the accident, Special Agent Crumwell arrived at the scene. Miraculously, no one had died, though there had been many serious injuries. Five ambulances were already on the scene. The traffic had slowed to a snail's pace.

Crumwell was promptly approached by the uniformed officer in charge and was given an account of what had happened.

"The air surveillance helicopter spotted Gregory leaving the truck which started this eighteen-car pileup. Then lost him."

Crumwell looked all around at the wrecked cars and removed his sunglasses. Then he frowned. "My God," he said. "What a mess this is. Anyone killed?"

"No," said the officer.

"Where is the driver of the truck?"

"We've got him cuffed and locked up."

"I want to see him," said Crumwell.

"Sure," said the officer as he led Crumwell to the police car a few yards ahead, on the side of the road.

Crumwell slipped his sunglasses into his inside coat pocket as he approached the police car. For a moment, he stared at the large bearded truck driver. The officer opened the rear door of the car and Crumwell sat in the back seat beside the truck driver, leaving the door open.

"My name is Crumwell," he said. "I'm with the FBI."

"And I just don't give a shit," the truck driver growled.

"His name is Jerry Tate," said the officer. "He's wanted in Texas for murder and robbery; possession of stolen property."

"Mr. Tate," said Crumwell, "I'm not concerned with what you did in Texas. My concern is with Steven Gregory, the man who was riding with you."

Crumwell could not help noticing the deep bleeding cut on the side of Tate's head where Gregory had struck him with the gun. "Where did he go after the accident?"

"How in the hell am I supposed to know?" Tate said. "That bastard hit me over the head with a gun; that's all I remember. Look, get me a doctor, will ya? I'm bleeding." Tate frowned and closed his eyes, as he leaned backward.

Crumwell got out of the car and walked to the pavement. He looked both ways, thoughtfully, down the road as far as his eyes could see.

The officer slammed the back door of the police car and joined Crumwell at the side of the road.

"Somebody had to have seen something," said Crumwell. "I want you to question everyone—everyone who was involved in the accident; and those curious watchers who had nothing better to do but just that. Your men have been issued pictures of Gregory. I want those pictures to be shown to everyone you talk to. Gregory didn't just vanish into thin air. He got out of the truck and probably got lost in the crowd that was gathering. He knew he was being watched. His only alternative was to hitch a ride by charm or by force. Now, the only question is: Which car?"

"I'll get on it," said the officer.

Less than five minutes later, a man in his late forties, with silver grey short hair approached a state trooper. The man had become a bit worried after he could not find his son. In addition, he had heard others in the immediate area state that the police were looking for an armed man who may have caused the accident.

"Officer, officer," said the man with the silver grey hair, "I can't find my son. He was driving a black Datsun. It's a 280Z. He wouldn't just drive off and leave me this way."

"What exactly are you saying, sir?" asked the officer.

"Well, I'd told my son to stop the car, because I wanted to try and help free a little girl and her mother from their car. I got so involved with everything, but now I can't find my son. He wouldn't just leave me here like this. I think something happened."

About twelve yards away, a state trooper was showing a photograph of Steven Gregory to a large woman wearing a straw hat.

"This man is armed and dangerous," the trooper said. "He is wanted by the FBI, and we know he was in the truck that started the accident."

"But look at the dent in my car," the woman said. "It's my sister's car and she's a real bitch. I'll never hear the end of it."

"Could you just look at the picture, please," said the state trooper.

The woman looked at that picture for a moment, and then said. "Hey, this looks like the man I saw earlier. He had a gun stuffed down in the front of his pants. He was standing no more than fourteen feet away from me at the time and I pulled my grandson close to me. I mean, it scared me. He was holding another gun in his hand."

"Did you notice where he went?"

"He got into one of those fancy little sports cars. I saw him."

"What color was the car?"

"It was black."

~~~~

The black Datsun was now traveling at a moderate pace down a road with much less traffic. Thick tall trees were on either side of the road. Gregory contemplated his next move.

"My name is Peter Winston," said the young man who was sitting behind the wheel. He appeared more relaxed now and Gregory was pleased with that fact. He didn't want the young driver to try anything stupid.

"Peter, I'm sorry I had to inconvenience you this way, but my life is on the line."

Peter smiled faintly. "Hey—no problem. Just tell me where you want to go."

"I won't need your services much longer," said Gregory looking through the rear window of the car.

They suddenly approached a small shopping center on the left side of the road; and a short distance ahead, a more heavily populated area with fast Food Restaurants, convenience stores, gas stations and other small businesses. And then there was only road again.

"You know," said Peter, "I really don't mind taking you where you want to go, but I wish I could let my dad know I'm okay. I know he'd be worried. We kind of left him back there at the sight of the accident. And knowing my father, he probably knows something is wrong."

"You mean you were not alone back there?" Gregory asked.

"No. I was not alone. I was with my dad."

Gregory started to feel uneasy. What if someone had seen him force his way into the car? Maybe the father saw his son drive off with some stranger. And what if the father had reported what he'd seen to the police at the scene of the accident? He could give the police a complete description of the car and even the license plate number. They are probably searching for the black Datsun right now, Gregory thought.

A motel was to the left of the road just ahead. Gregory spotted it. As they passed by the motel, Gregory looked all about the immediate area. When they were about a tenth of a mile past the motel, Gregory said "Okay, pull over and stop the car."

Peter Winston complied with Gregory's request. When the car stopped, Gregory grabbed the gun from between his feet and got out of the car. "I want you to get out of here, quick!" Then he slammed the door shut and slapped the roof of the car. "Get out of here."

Within seconds, the black Datsun was out of sight. Gregory shoved the second gun under his waistband and covered them both with his jacket. Then he started to jog back down the road to the motel. He had instructed the young driver to pull over to the side of the road a distance from the motel because he wanted to give the impression that he would just hitch another ride. It was just a precautionary measure, just in case the police would question the driver of the Datsun. Gregory didn't want young Peter Winston to tell the police that he dropped him off in front of the Pink Dove Motel, especially since Gregory intended to hide out there for a while.

The Pink Dove Motel was not one of the better motels around, but under the circumstances, Gregory could not be choosy. At least it was better than nothing at all. And it was certainly better than the open forest where he'd spent the previous night.

Getting a room had not been a problem. The attendant at the desk was a woman in her late fifties who wore heavy makeup and a pink dress. What else would the owner of the 'Pink' Dove Motel be wearing anyway, Gregory thought.

"I own this joint, honey," she told Gregory, after she gave him the key to his room. "So if you have any problems, you come see me." Her breath was whiskey thick, but she seemed to be in full control of her mental faculties. She had not seen Gregory pull up in a car, nor did she see him carrying a suitcase. Yet, she was not suspicious. It was not unusual, for The Pink Dove Motel was known as a clandestine rendezvous where men and women came often to cheat on their spouses.

Gregory's room number was eight. He slipped the key into the keyhole and turned the key clockwise. He then turned and looked about the parking area and noticed only one car parked three doors down. He unlocked the door and entered the room quickly.

He had paid the woman at the desk twenty-five dollars. He had only six dollars left in his pocket.

For a moment, Gregory stood silently, leaning backward against the closed door. Then he moved to the window to see if he could see anyone who looked suspicious. He was paranoid and with good reason, considering what he'd experienced in the last forty-eight hours.

Through the window, he could see the parking area clearly. To the right was the road. For a moment he watched anxiously, but not one car drove by.

He sighed deeply. He was relieved. At least for now he felt safe. He removed both guns from underneath his jacket and tossed them onto the bed. The room had a stale odor but it was much neater than he had expected, judging from the outside of the building which was poor and rundown.

Gregory moved to the bathroom and stopped in front of the mirror. Only then did he notice the scratches and bruises on his face sustained during the previous night as he blindly tackled the trees and bushes of the woods. He was surprised that the attendant at the desk didn't make any comments about his face.

He turned the tap water on and watched the water flow into the sink. As the cold and hot water mixed, he grabbed the bar of soap, put his hands under the flow and washed his face. He dropped the bar of soap then rinsed his face. He reached for the adjacent towel and dried his face. The towel felt rough, and did not smell clean.

Gregory dropped the towel on the floor and unzipped his jacket. Once again, he was reminded of how close he had come to death on the previous night in that phone booth, as he waited for a return call from his Uncle Max. The large blood stain on his shirt was completely dry and it felt uncomfortable against his skin. He started to feel sick as he thought of that dead man lying on top of him.

Gregory shivered with weakness and suddenly leaned forward against the sink, trying to brace himself. He thought he might vomit, but he did not. He took deep breaths in an attempt to pull himself back together.

Abruptly he left the bathroom and walked toward the bed. He felt so tired and so sleepy. He sat on the edge of the squeaky bed and stared aimlessly at the pink wall in front of him. He smiled faintly and thought. Why not? *Pink* walls are appropriate for the "Pink" Dove Motel.

Gregory shook his head suddenly from side to side, then stretched out on the bed and fell asleep.

Later when Gregory awoke, there was darkness all around him. He sat up in bed. He had slept right through the remainder of the day and into the night. He pressed the little "light" button on his wristwatch and learned that it was almost 8:30 PM. He was drenched with perspiration and his heart was pounding as his body trembled uncontrollably. He'd had a bad dream about his wife, Freda.

In the dream, he saw his wife lying in her hospital bed looking up at him. Her hands were reaching out for him as she smiled and said. "I love you." Suddenly his wife found it difficult to breathe.

Then Gregory was pinned against the wall by three doctors as his wife was being wheeled out of the room as she lay on her bed. He saw her reacting violently. Someone had placed a pillow over her face and was pressing down firmly. Gregory could not see the face of the person who was smothering his wife. He could see only the large hands of a man pressing down on the pillow as his wife's hands grabbed frantically at the void. The IV bottle clanged against the post, and her feet kicked the covers from her body as she was wheeled rapidly down the long corridor to an elevator.

Gregory awoke with tears in his eyes. "God, she can't be dead. Don't let her be dead."

They had not even had children yet, Gregory thought. They had married when they were young. They had both been in their mid-twenties at the time and had only recently started giving parenthood some very serious consideration. Gregory had often wondered if his wife's interests in the daycare center—working constantly with little children—had influenced her.

Gregory and his wife had so much going for them. They lived in a nice neighborhood and a beautiful home. Great friends. Gregory's firm was doing well. He and his wife were in the very best of health and were ready to start a family. And most of all, they truly loved each other.

But now, the beauty and the dreams were shattered. Gregory hopped out of bed and walked over to the window of the motel room and looked outside into the darkness. A neon sign advertising the vacancies at the Pink Dove Motel stood tall in front of the building near the office. The parking area of the motel was not very well lighted. Only two lampposts strategically located provided meager light for the outside of the motel.

The entire motel was in the form of a horseshoe, with most of the rooms facing each other and with the parking area in the middle of the horseshoe-shaped area; a parking space was in front of almost each room.

Across from him, Gregory noticed a man and a woman leaving their room. The man had a handful of the woman's hair when he pushed her toward his car. The two were involved in a heated verbal dispute. Gregory hoped that the two would calm down. He hated to think of what might happen if the woman at the desk heard the shouting and called the police. A policeman was the last person that Gregory wanted to see.

For nearly three minutes, the altercation continued. Finally the man forced the woman into the car and they drove away. Gregory was relieved. He moved back over to the bed and sat on the edge of it. He was even uneasy about turning on the nearby television set. He wanted to be able to hear any and everything.

Gregory stretched out on the bed once again. He still felt rather tired and he wanted to relax a bit longer. But he fell asleep suddenly and did not wake up anymore that night. In fact, it was not until a couple of moments before 6:00 AM that he opened his eyes again.

He thought that he'd been dreaming when he felt that hard cold object touching his forehead. When he opened his eyes, he saw the sunlight glimmering through the cheap curtains at the window and he froze. His pulse rate raced. A man with a slender build and a clean shaven, expressionless face was staring down at him. He had a gun pressed against Gregory's forehead.

The slender man who held the gun to Gregory's head was the cold-blooded killer who had been paid twenty thousand dollars by FBI Inspector Miller to murder the ex-football player. His name was Carl Hilderbrant.

~~~~

At the restaurant only a couple of miles up the road from the Pink Dove Motel, two well-dressed men wearing suits had just finished having breakfast at a table near the front window.

"Where could that bastard be?" said the man who wore the brown suit.

"That kid who drove Gregory from the accident scene told the police that he dropped Gregory off in this general area," said the other.

"We've been showing Gregory's picture to everyone and no-body has seen him. I think we're wasting our time. He probably forced his way into someone else's car at gunpoint *again* and is miles away from here now."

"You might be right but we don't have any clues to go on. It's a long shot for sure but we have to keep checking. Hopefully, someone saw him. Gregory is a smart man. But he has to eat and he has to sleep. We must keep looking and asking. Maybe we will get lucky."

The man wearing the brown suit sipped at his coffee. "Okay, so we've asked around at the shopping center, the gas stations and the fast food restaurants—customers and employees. Where do we check next?"

"We'll continue up the road a bit further; see what we can find. Let's go."

The two men rose from the table and left the restaurant. Outside, they walked to their car and got inside. The man who wore the brown suit sat behind the wheel and started up the car's engine. In a moment, they pulled out of the restaurant parking area to the road.

They approached the Pink Dove Motel and the driver reduced the speed of the car at his partner's request.

"The motel on the left," he said. "Let's check it out."

"Okay," said the driver. He pulled the car off the road and parked near the motel office.

Both of the men got out of the car and entered the office. The elderly woman dressed in pink sat behind the desk.

"And what can I do for you gentlemen?" The woman asked.

The man who wore the brown suit reached into his coat pocket and pulled out a picture of Steven Gregory and placed it on the desk. "We are government agents," he said. "Have you seen this man within the last twenty-four hours?"

The woman behind the desk grabbed the picture from the desk and looked at it for a moment, then looked back up at the two men and paused.

Chapter 6

CARL HILDERBRANT REMOVED his gun from Gregory's head and took a couple of steps backward, after he pushed the two guns beside Gregory to the floor.

Gregory was speechless as he stared into the barrel of the forty-four. He felt certain that he was going to die.

"Don't be alarmed, Mr. Gregory," said Hilderbrant. "I was hired by your uncle to protect you." He lowered his gun.

Gregory slowly sat up in bed. "Uncle Max hired you to protect me? How did you find me?"

"The police questioned the college student who drove you away from the eighteen-car accident yesterday. In a nutshell, Mr. Gregory, I did my home-work. Through my sources within the FBI, I learned of the statement that the college student made. He dropped you off in this general area. It didn't take me long to figure out that you had only two options: either you'd hitch another ride by force and take the chance of falling asleep or doing something reckless with your gun while holding someone hostage—which is contrary to your established character, by the way—or you'd do something sensible, like hiding out here at this motel for a while, until you were rested."

"Okay," said Gregory. "So you've found me."

"And that was pretty clever of you signing in at the desk as Robert Turner. I knew it was your handwriting the moment I saw the name."

Gregory stared at Hilderbrant with amazement. And he admitted to himself that the slender man who stood before him really knew his stuff. Gregory felt as though his life was an open book at that moment. And he wondered what else Hilderbrant knew about him.

"So, what do we do now?" Gregory asked.

"First, we get you out of here," said Hilderbrant. "It won't take very long for the Federal boys to consider the possibility of your presence here." He moved to the window and parted the curtains slightly. "Well, no time to lose now. We have company."

Gregory rose quickly from the bed. "Police?"

"No," said Hilderbrant. "This guy might be a government agent." Hilderbrant saw one of the men leave the office with haste, move to his car and start to talk on the radio. "He's probably calling for back-up."

"We've got to get out of here," said Gregory.

"My car is the black one out front," said Hilderbrant. "The key is in the ignition. Stay here until I start shooting, then make a run for the car and pick me up."

"Okay," said Gregory as he watched Hilderbrant leave the room.

Gregory closed the door and stood very still. In a moment he heard the sound of gunfire. He opened the door quickly, ran out of the room to the car out front, and jumped behind the wheel. He started up the engine and sped off backward, then stopped. He then turned the wheel and started forward toward Hilderbrant, who was standing in the doorway of the office, looking down at the man who wore the brown suit. Hilderbrant had shot the man once in the chest.

The woman who sat behind the desk was screaming hysterically.

As Hilderbrant ran toward Gregory, the ex-football player noticed a large gunshot hole in the windshield of the car that the two men had pulled up in. The second man was leaning backward against the seat with a fatal head wound.

Hilderbrant quickly jumped into the car driven by Gregory and they quickly left the Pink Dove Motel.

"It seems you have more than just the FBI interested in you," said Hilderbrant, as they drove along the road.

"What do you mean?" Gregory asked.

"Those were not FBI agents back there. I recognized the one in the doorway. He's a member of a CIA hit squad."

Gregory frowned. "The CIA?"

"What exactly is it that you have that everyone wants?"

"You mean, you don't know?" said Gregory. "I was hoping that you could tell me."

"My job is to keep you alive. That's all I know—that's all they wanted me to know."

"And who are 'they'?"

"Your uncle, of course; and his associates"

There was a pause.

Then Gregory said, "I have to contact my uncle."

They drove nearly nine miles before Gregory spotted a pay phone near the curb in front of a gas station. Both Gregory and Hilderbrant got out of the car.

Gregory moved to the telephone and removed the receiver. As he dialed his uncle's home phone number, Hilderbrant watched over Gregory's shoulder. He memorized the numbers being dialed. Realizing that the call was long distance, Gregory hung up with a slam and said, "Damn, I need operator assistance."

"Here," said Hilderbrant, reaching into his inside coat pocket. "Use my phone card." He reached Gregory his telephone card.

When Gregory finally got his call through, he learned that his uncle had left a message on his telephone answering machine. On the portion of the tape—the outgoing message—instructing the caller to leave a message at the sound of the beep, Gregory received a very shocking message from his Uncle Max: "Steven, this is your Uncle Max. By the time you hear this message, I will be dead."

Gregory sighed deeply as he trembled with anguish, but he kept the receiver pressed to his ear and listened to the message, the voice of his uncle: "You have what they want, Steven. I'm sorry I had to involve you, but I had no choice. Use it to your advantage: The British Concord; my estate in Cal—"

The tape had ended and Gregory slowly removed the receiver from his ear and dropped it as he turned away from the phone and started to walk back toward the car.

Hilderbrant knew that something was wrong. He followed Gregory back to the car and watched as he sat behind the wheel.

"What did you find out?" asked Hilderbrant.

"My uncle is dead," said Gregory.

~~~~

Later that morning, Gregory and Hilderbrant went to the motel where Hilderbrant was staying. It was about a twenty-mile drive from the Pink Dove Motel. It was a great deal cleaner and was equipped with a swimming pool. It was a Holiday Inn.

Gregory showered and shaved while Hilderbrant went after hamburgers. Hilderbrant had offered Gregory one of his pullover knit shirts so that he could get rid of the awful smelling blood-stained shirt that Gregory had worn for a couple of days. Since there was a difference in their physique, the shirt fitted Gregory rather tightly. He had to settle for the pants which he'd worn for the past couple of days because he could not fit into a pair of Hilderbrant's slacks.

Even in their new location, it was dangerous for Gregory. Hilderbrant had pointed this out to him when he had returned to the room with the hamburgers. He had noticed a suspicious-looking character hanging around the main entrance of the building.

"We can't stay here," Hilderbrant said to Gregory, as he entered the room. "Call it instincts, call it what you want. Government agents are all over the place."

~~~~

Special Agent Crumwell arrived at the Pink Dove Motel shortly after 10 AM that morning. From the elderly woman who owned the motel, Crumwell learned that Steven Gregory had checked into the motel on the previous day.

"And now," the owner of the motel had said, "first thing this morning, these two guys come in here and tell me that they are government agents and they show me a picture of some guy that they are looking for. I told them that the man in the picture was here. Then one of the two men ran outside to his car, while the other one stayed and started asking me which room was the man in the picture occupying. Then I told him it was room number eight. Then I heard two shots fired outside. And before I knew what had happened, the guy who I was talking to opened the door, and he got shot in the chest."

"Did the man in the picture do the shooting?" asked Crumwell.

"No. It was a smaller man. Slender. He had just checked in to the motel about twenty minutes before those two government agents pulled up."

"And what was his name?"

"He signed in as Tom Harris. I thought there was something strange about him. After he'd signed his name, he took his time reading all of the other names on the list. When I asked him what he was doing, he just kind of smiled and said he thought he recognized a friend's name."

"The man in the picture," said Crumwell. "Did you see him leave?"

"No. I only saw the slender man jump into a car and someone drove him away."

"Did you see who was driving the car?"

"No."

"What was the color of the car?"

"I don't remember exactly. Everything was happening so fast. I was so scared. I think it was a dark color."

Crumwell felt certain that the man who was driving that car was Steven Gregory. But who was the slender man who had helped Gregory to escape? Only a few moments later, word came over

Crumwell's car radio that Steven Gregory had been spotted at a Holiday Inn motel and that he and one other unidentified man were cornered in a room and the area was being sealed off.

When Crumwell arrived at the Holiday Inn, he saw two FBI air surveillance helicopters in the sky. Numerous FBI agents were already on the scene, stationed at strategic locations, with their guns on the ready.

After nearly thirty minutes of conflicting reports about the exact location of Gregory, the agents and the police moved into the room where they believed Gregory was. They found his blood-stained shirt on the floor of the bathroom and two hamburgers in a bag on the top of the bed. Steven Gregory and Carl Hilderbrant were gone.

~~~~

About seventeen miles away, later that evening, Steven Gregory stood silently at the window of a tenth-floor apartment, looking down at the automobile traffic. It was Hilderbrant's two bedroom apartment, overlooking San Francisco.

Gregory and Hilderbrant had made a very narrow escape from the Holiday Inn by forcing an elderly couple to leave with them. As Gregory and Hilderbrant were leaving their room, the elderly couple was just returning to theirs, after spending nearly an hour relaxing around the swimming pool. Before the husband could reach the doorknob to enter their room, Hilderbrant grabbed the man's wrist and said "I need some wheels. Cooperate with me."

When the man saw Hilderbrant's gun, he said. "Please don't hurt us. I'll do anything you want. Just name it."

"Take us to your car," said Hilderbrant. The elderly couple complied.

Gregory and Hilderbrant followed them downstairs to the parking area where all four of them got into the elderly couple's fancy green Cadillac. The couple sat in the front seat, with the husband behind the wheel, while Gregory and Hilderbrant hopped into the back seat and lowered their heads so that no one could see them. Then Hilderbrant had instructed the man to drive at the normal rate of speed.

After they were about a block away from the Holiday Inn, Gregory and Hilderbrant sat up and had looked through the rear window, as government cars pulled into the motel parking area quickly. They could see police cars in the distance behind them getting ready to block the road off.

Gregory now sighed as he stood near the window in Hilderbrant's apartment, remembering that most recent close call.

But his thoughts suddenly shifted to the tape recorded message made by his uncle: "By the time you hear this message, I will be dead."

There was no way of knowing if his Uncle Max were truly dead at that moment, but Gregory felt certain that his uncle was sure that he would soon be killed.

Maxwell Craving was his last living relative and it was difficult for Gregory to suppress his sadness. First it was his wife; then his best friend Alvin. And now, Uncle Max.

So now he was on his own, Gregory thought. All he had left was Hilderbrant, who was quietly alone in the adjacent bedroom. But how much did he really know about that man, other than the fact that he was a clever man who would not hesitate to kill. It was time for Gregory to pull himself together and review his situation.

And he did. First, he considered that his Uncle Max had retired from the FBI a year ago and had remained living in Washington, D.C. He had been the director of the FBI.

Gregory thought that his own problem had something to do with a *big case* that his uncle was working on sometime before his retirement. His uncle had told him *that* much when he'd phoned him the second time on the night that Gregory was nearly gunned down in that telephone booth.

Gregory's uncle had also said that the FBI was not what it used to be, and that things had changed within the system, and that there was an *internal struggle* going on. Was the FBI becoming, or had it become, an autonomous group similar to the underworld? The Mafia? That would be ridiculous, Gregory thought. Certainly not the FBI.

Then what could it be?

Next point, Gregory considered: the FBI wanted him dead; and why? Because they *thought* he knew too much about the case that his Uncle Max had been working on. And why would they think that Gregory knew too much? The answer was simple, Gregory thought. The FBI assumed that his Uncle Max had sent him the computer disk which would probably explain why everyone was so interested in obtaining it in the first place. And the FBI probably also assumed that his Uncle Max revealed the *contents* of the disk to Gregory, which meant that Gregory was now a high risk.

But Gregory had not received any disk from his uncle. So why would the FBI think that he had? Perhaps his uncle had told them so. But that would be a lie, Gregory thought, because he never received the disk.

Hilderbrant had recognized one of the men at the Pink Dove Motel as being a member of a CIA hit squad. Did that suggest that the CIA, as well as the FBI, had a stake in the disk? Perhaps the scope of the mystery was far greater than his Uncle Max had hinted.

Hilderbrant suddenly came out of his bedroom and joined Gregory in the living room. "I've just checked with my source in Washington," he said. "Your uncle is indeed missing. Has been for nearly twenty-four hours."

"That doesn't have to mean that he's actually dead," Gregory said.

"That's true," said Hilderbrant, "but I wouldn't count on it."

There was a pause.

And Gregory said, "So what do we do now?"

"Why don't we start by you leveling with me, Mr. Gregory? Why don't you tell me what it is that you have that everyone is looking for?"

"From what I can gather, they want some computer disk that I know nothing about. And I think perhaps you should level with me a bit, too. You told me that your name is Hilderbrant. Yet, the name on the telephone card that you gave me at the pay phone is Tom Harris."

Hilderbrant smiled faintly and said, "You're very observant, Mr. Gregory. You see, in my line of business, it doesn't pay to keep one name for a very long period of time."

"And what exactly is your line of business? And how do you know my uncle? You told me that my uncle hired you to protect me."

"I worked for your uncle when he was the director of the FBI. I'm in the extermination business. I've made some hits for the FBI; the CIA. Your uncle knew I was in town on business. He contacted me and requested that I help. He told me that you were in danger, and that he wanted me to help you stay alive. He told me that he would give me the details later, but he never got the chance. Your uncle was a very powerful man when he was director of the FBI."

"He never mentioned the disk to you?" Gregory asked.

"No," said Hilderbrant.

Gregory moved from the window and started toward Hilderbrant. "Uncle Max was trying to tell me something—that recorded message that he left on his answering machine. He was speaking in a code. It was a game we used to play when I was a kid. I think he was trying to tell me the location of the disk."

"What exactly did he say?" said Hilderbrant.

"He said: 'the British Concorde; my estate in Cal—'"

There was a pause.

"Is that it?" said Hilderbrant.

"Yes," Gregory answered. "He was referring to his estate in California. 'Cal' meant California. The message on the tape ran out before he could give me more clues."

"What would the British Concorde or his estate in California have to do with the location of the disk?"

"I don't know," Gregory answered. "I was never very good at his secret code game."

"Well, whatever info there is recorded on that disk has to be very valuable to a lot of people. I was paid a very hefty sum of money to murder you."

"What is that supposed to mean," asked Gregory

Hilderbrant moved to the adjacent bar, atop which rested a briefcase. He opened the briefcase so that Gregory could see the contents. "This is twenty thousand dollars in cash, as you can see. All one hundred dollar bills. The local FBI inspector, Anthony

Miller, paid me this amount in advance. I will receive twenty thousand more after I bring them your dead body. That's a total of forty thousand dollars."

Gregory stood speechless as he stared at the money. "Is Miller the head man?" he asked.

"He's not the number one man. But he has a great deal of power. Even on a national scale."

"My wife disappeared from the hospital two days ago. Do you think this man would know what happened to her?"

"Miller is the man who would know," Hilderbrant said.

Gregory turned away from him and moved back to the window and stared thoughtfully. "What do you think about a trade off?" he asked. He faced Hilderbrant. "My wife for the disk. Sure, they want me dead because they *think* I know too much. But I'll bet they'd want the disk even more."

"There are two problems with that plan," Hilderbrant pointed out. "First, there's no guarantee that your wife is still alive. Second, you don't have the disk."

"But they don't know that. As far as they are concerned, I've just been unwilling to cooperate with them. Even the guy who I shot in the restaurant two days ago hinted to me that they'd do *anything in their power* to get that disk. At the very least, I could find out if my wife is still alive."

"Then what if she *is* a live? And you can't come up with the disk. They'd kill her for sure."

"They'd kill her for 'sure' if they had no further 'use' for her. And how do I know if making a tradeoff wasn't their original plan anyway. Maybe that was the reason for taking my wife in the first place. So tell me, do you know how to contact this Miller guy? Can you call him?"

"I can do better than that," said Hilderbrant. "I can meet with him face to face. Besides, I've already received twenty thousand dollars. I should at least do some work for 'somebody'." He smiled faintly as he moved back to the bar and closed the briefcase which contained the twenty thousand dollars.

Chapter 7

FBI INSPECTOR ANTHONY Miller sat at a table in his favorite restaurant, smoking a Cuban cigar, on that night of February 6. He had arrived a couple of moments after seven. It was now a quarter after the hour. But he didn't mind the wait, for he had received a call earlier from Carl Hilderbrant, who wanted to arrange a meeting.

Miller felt at ease and less tense because, as a rule, Hilderbrant would *never* contact him after accepting a job, unless the job had been completed. Miller felt confident that Steven Gregory had been exterminated. He was so confident, in fact, that he had brought along with him a briefcase which contained the other half of Hilderbrant's pay: an extra twenty thousand in cash.

Miller spotted Hilderbrant, walking slowly toward him. He took a sip from his drink, and then drew in smoke from his cigar.

When Hilderbrant approached the table, he frowned faintly as he closed his eyes. "Why did you light up a cigar?" he said as he removed a handkerchief from his coat pocket. "You knew I was coming." He covered his nose with the handkerchief.

"I'm sorry," said Miller with insincerity. "He smothered the tip of the cigar in the ashtray on the table as Hilderbrant sat down directly across from him.

Miller placed the briefcase on the table and asked, "Did you finish the job?"

"Not quite," Hilderbrant said in his usual calm manner, with an expressionless face.

Miller grew very serious. "What do you mean, not quite?"

"I've been thinking about the money that you're paying me to exterminate Gregory. Forty thousand dollars is an awful lot of money to pay for one hit. That disk must be very valuable."

"How did you find out about the disk?" Miller had become very excited now.

"I've got Gregory," said Hilderbrant, "and he is the only person who knows the location of the disk."

"You were supposed to kill him. We had a deal."

"But now, it's a new ball game, Tony—do you mind if I call you Tony? After nearly eight years of doing business together, I think we should be on a first name basis, don't you think?" Hilderbrant returned his handkerchief to his coat pocket.

There was a pause.

"Where is Gregory?" Miller asked.

"He's in a safe place. Gregory wants his wife in exchange for the disk."

"And what if I can't deliver his wife?"

Hilderbrant smiled faintly and responded. "Then you'd have a problem. But I know you 'can' deliver her because I know you were not dumb enough to hurt her."

There was a pause.

Miller's face had guilt written all over it.

"But on the other hand," Hilderbrant continued, "if you 'were' stupid enough to dispose of her—not to worry. That's where I come in. I will convince Gregory that his wife is still alive. Gregory is the only person who knows the location of the disk. It will be an even trade. Gregory will get his wife and you will get the disk. It's all very simple. But—"

"But what?" Miller interrupted.

"I'm convinced that the disk is worth much more than the forty thousand that you're paying me to exterminate Gregory. I think it's only fair that I be paid a bit more since I'm going to be the mediator."

"How much more?" Miller asked.

"Well, I'm not greedy. Let's say one flat figure—one that we can all live with. Let's say one hundred thousand dollars."

"You won't get away with this, Hilderbrant. You're crazy. And on top of that, you are a dead man."

Hilderbrant slowly shifted his stare downward and then calmly looked at Miller and said, "Tony—you know me; you've heard of me. You know my reputation. Now, some way, somehow, I'll get what I want. I will use the disk to destroy you and your superiors— whoever they might be."

Hilderbrant leaned forward on the table toward Miller. "It would be in your best interest to keep me alive. Because I 'can' get the disk for you. But you will have to cooperate with me."

"My people won't like this."

"I'm an independent, Tony," Hilderbrant said placidly. "I will still be able to find work when this is all over."

"I'll have to contact my superiors," Miller said. "One hundred thousand dollars is a lot of money." He suddenly finished his drink with one swallow. And as he placed the empty glass on the table, his hand trembled uncontrollably.

"It'll work out, Tony," Hilderbrant offered. "Don't worry. You just convince your people to see things my way." Hilderbrant rose from the table. "I will contact you within a couple of hours. You 'will have' talked to your superiors by then—with favorable results to share with me, I'm sure."

Hilderbrant started to walk away but Miller called his name and said. "Convince Gregory that his wife is alive. And that he has twenty-four hours to give us what we want."

Hilderbrant stared at Miller for a moment, and then he turned and left the restaurant.

~~~~

Miller moved promptly. First he contacted his superiors in Washington, D.C., and conveyed to them the problem with Hilderbrant and his demands. Then Miller called Special Agent Crumwell from the field to have a meeting with him.

Anthony Miller sat behind the desk in his office, while special agent Crumwell sat in the armchair in front of the desk, facing the nervous inspector.

A glass filled with brandy was on Miller's desk. The inspector had been sipping at the brandy constantly since the meeting began. He had been perspiring profusely since he'd ended the conversation with his superiors in Washington. He had removed his necktie and unbuttoned the collar of his shirt. "Hilderbrant has been helping Gregory to stay one step ahead of us for too long," Miller said. "Do you realize what could happen if the disk falls into the wrong hands?"

Crumwell watched silently as Miller buried his face in his hands and sighed as he massaged his eyes.

"Washington has issued new orders," said Miller. "I want you to contact all of your field agents and tell them the following: Carl Hilderbrant is to be eliminated immediately. That bastard was hired to help us—now he's attempting to blackmail us. Washington would rather we take our chances with Gregory. Hilderbrant is a professional. He could hurt us a lot more than Gregory could if he got the disk."

"Then we will have to communicate with Gregory directly," said agent Crumwell.

"Exactly," said Miller. "He thinks he can trade the disk for his wife. Hilderbrant says he knows where Gregory is. Do you think he's bluffing?"

"Gregory made a very narrow escape twice today. And we are sure he was assisted by a tall man with a slender build, which fits Hilderbrant's description. I think Hilderbrant knows exactly where Gregory is."

"Okay, then," said Miller. "Notify your men at once."

"But what about the CIA hit squad. They have orders to hit Gregory on sight."

"The CIA has its own reasons for wanting Gregory dead. I'll see what I can do. But Gregory is 'not' to die until after we get the disk. Those are our new orders. If the CIA hit squad jeopardizes our operation, then we must take appropriate action against them."

~~~~

By nine forty-five that night, Special Agent Crumwell had assembled twelve of his chief agents in a room adjacent to inspector

Miller's Office. The men sat at a long table—six men on either side of Agent Crumwell who stood at the head of the table, operating a slide projector.

"You are familiar with Steven Gregory," said Crumwell, as a picture of Gregory appeared on the screen. "He is believed to be in or near the Oakland or San Francisco Bay areas. All you have to know about his psychological profile is that he is generally a compassionate man. But he won't hesitate to shoot if he feels threatened. Currently, it is believed that he is heavily armed—since he's met this man."

A picture of Carl Hilderbrant flashed on the screen.

"His name is Carl Hilderbrant," said Crumwell. "Or at least that's the name he uses most often. Or as *he* puts it, it's his 'professional' name. Like an author's pen name. No one knows his real name. He changes his name constantly. Dozens of aliases. He has a visa for each name."

Next slide.

"Unless he's about to make a hit, he stays away from crowded places like nightclubs and bars. He hates the smell of tobacco smoke and he doesn't drink alcoholic beverages. So now we know the places where we don't have to look for him."

Next slide.

"Whenever he moves to a new city, he immediately, through his underworld chain of connections, gains access to no less than six apartments, ranging from the most expensive high-rises to some of the cheapest motels. He does this because he always needs a new place to hide and he also feels that this *system* minimizes the chance of his being staked out."

Next slide.

"No one knows where he's from originally, or when or where he was born. His age range is 29 to 34. He is wanted by several countries for numerous reasons ranging from spying to assassination. He has worked for the CIA, the KGB, the FBI, and the Mafia. He has been nicknamed the Killing Machine."

Next slide.

"He is a con man; double agent; a professional killer for hire."

The next slide which appeared on the screen was the actual murder of a CIA agent by Hilderbrant.

"This is an actual clip of a stakeout video. Hilderbrant was acting as a courier in Germany two years ago. The man sitting in the car, whose brain you see being splattered all over the seats, was a CIA agent."

Next slide.

"Hilderbrant is a cold-blooded killer with liquid nitrogen flowing through his veins instead of blood. He is heavily armed with automatic weapons and a high-powered rifle for long-range executions—his favorite weapon for assassinations. Hilderbrant is to be exterminated on site."

Next slide.

"Our immediate area of concentration will be in and around apartment buildings, motels. Hilderbrant is at his best when he works alone. But he now has Gregory tagging along. Hopefully, he will be slowed down a bit and he'll make some mistakes."

~~~~

In a hotel bedroom about two miles from the restaurant where he had met with Inspector Miller earlier, Hilderbrant reached for the tape recorder on the dresser. Then he sat on the edge of the bed. With the miniature recorder in his hands, Hilderbrant pressed the button that allowed the tape to rewind, until it stopped automatically, at the beginning of the tape.

Then he picked up the receiver of the nearby phone and recalled the numbers which he had seen Gregory dial earlier that day at the pay phone, near a gas station, when he was trying to reach his Uncle Max in Washington.

Hilderbrant dialed Maxwell Craven's home number in Washington. Then he pressed the "record" button on the tape recorder and placed the microphone to the earpiece of the receiver and recorded the outgoing message from Craven's answering machine.

After recording the message, Hilderbrant hung up and pressed the "stop" button on the recorder. He rewinded the tape and played back the recorded message intended for Gregory: "Steven, this is your Uncle Max. By the time you hear this message, I will be dead. You have what they want, Steven. I'm sorry I had to involve you, but I had no choice. Use it to your advantage: The British Concorde; my estate in Cal—"

The tape ended.

Hilderbrant sat silently and stared ahead thoughtfully.

Chapter 8

STEVEN GREGORY PACED anxiously about the living room in the apartment as he awaited the return of Carl Hilderbrant. He hoped that everything would go well and that his wife was alive and had not been harmed.

Hilderbrant had been gone for nearly two hours, and Gregory had become very impatient. He went out onto the balcony, and for a moment, stared out at the darkness. It was peaceful and quiet on the tenth floor. There was a pleasant breeze, but Gregory soon became tired of the view and returned inside. He noticed the door to Hilderbrant's bedroom had been left open.

Gregory moved to the bedroom door and looked into the room. Everything was neat and orderly. The bed had been made but Gregory noticed something strange on the bed. There was a high-powered rifle complete with telescope, an eighteen-inch automatic weapon and the briefcase which contained the twenty thousand dollars which Hilderbrant had been paid to kill Gregory. But the thing which appeared to be most strange to Gregory was the tiny object in front of the closed briefcase. He moved closer to the bed and closer, until he was within two feet of the bed. He frowned with his mouth partially agape. The tiny object which he saw was a grenade. And even more shocking, behind the briefcase was a wide belt which resembled a utility belt. The belt, which could be worn about the waist, was stretched out on the bed with five grenades attached to it.

Hilderbrant was prepared for war, Gregory thought. He concluded that Hilderbrant must be some kind of terrorist. Maybe Hilderbrant was on the level when he admitted that he'd worked as a hit man for the FBI and CIA.

An abrupt ring.

The telephone in the living room was ringing.

Gregory hesitated for a moment, debating whether or not he should answer the phone. But he finally went to the living room and picked up the receiver after the eight ring. He put the receiver to his ear, but did not speak a word.

"It's okay, Gregory," said the voice on the other end of the wire. "It's Hilderbrant."

"Hilderbrant," said Gregory. "How did it go?"

"I talked to Miller. He said you have twenty-four hours to come up with the disk."

"But what about my wife? Is she okay? Where is she?"

"She's okay."

"How do you know that?" Gregory asked. "Did you see her?"

"Of course not," Hilderbrant answer. "But I'm convinced she's alive. He knows how I do business. He knows he won't get the disk unless your wife is alive. I made that very clear to him. You'll have to trust me. Miller and I have a mutual respect for each other. I'm positive that your wife is alive and well. She's valuable to them in terms of a trade-off. You've got to believe me. They never intended to hurt your wife."

There was a pause.

Gregory thought for a moment. He closed his eyes and bit downward on his lower lip.

"Gregory, are you still there?" Hilderbrant asked.

"Yes," said Gregory. "I'm still here. But I don't know where the disk is."

"You've got to think, Gregory. You told me yourself that your uncle was trying to tell you something in that taped message on his telephone answering machine."

"I know that, and I believe he 'was' trying to tell me something."

"It's in your hands, Gregory," said Hilderbrant. "You've got twenty-four hours."

"Where are you?" asked Gregory.

"I'm in a hotel room. I have access to more than one. Miller knows that I'm hiding you. I couldn't take the risk of joining you there. There's a chance I could have been followed by Miller's people. But don't worry—you're safe. Just remember, you must have the disk by eight o'clock tomorrow night or it's all over."

"How will I contact them?" Gregory asked.

"You won't have to," Hilderbrant answered. "I will be the courier."

"Well, how will I contact 'you'?"

"You won't have to. *I* will contact *you*."

The dial tone.

Hilderbrant had hung up.

"Wait!" Gregory shouted. "Don't—damn!" He hung up with a slam.

He sighed deeply, then moved to the sofa and dropped his body down on it. He was faced with a dilemma which could ultimately cause the death of his wife as well as his own. He was absolutely furious with Hilderbrant for hanging up the phone so soon. Gregory had wanted more details.

But now Gregory realized that he had to trust Hilderbrant to call him back. He covered his face with his hands and leaned backward on the sofa. With a slow movement, he dragged his hands downward off his face, as his head leaned backward over the back of the sofa. Now he was staring aimlessly at the ceiling.

He recalled the taped message on his uncle's telephone answering machine. He couldn't recall the taped message verbatim, only bits of it: "You have what they want, Steven ... British Concorde; my estate in Cal—"

As a child, Gregory and his uncle played a word game using special codes to solve riddles. And that's what he thought his uncle was using in the recorded telephone message. The secret code was a way of *speaking* so that Gregory and his uncle could communicate, in the presence of others, but only Gregory and his uncle would know what they were 'really' saying to each other.

For example, in the sentence from the tape recorded message: "The British Concorde," Gregory knew that the key word was "Concorde," because Concorde was the *last word of the sentence*. And that was the rule. The beginning of the sentence was meant to confuse the untrained ear.

"Concorde" was the key word, Gregory thought. But in the second clue, Gregory thought his uncle had broken the rule. "My estate in California." The word *California* seemed to be too general. Gregory reasoned finally that sure, it was true that his uncle had an estate in California. But what connection did his estate in California have with the word "Concorde"?

Gregory admitted to himself that he was never very good with that silly word game. And he was sure that his uncle would have given him more clues as to the location of the disk that everyone was looking for, but he just simply ran out of time. So now Gregory had to go it alone.

Shortly after midnight, after hours of trying to determine what his uncle was really trying to say in that recorded message, Gregory's eyelids had begun to grow heavier and heavier. He had found an ink pen and note pad on the counter in the kitchen and had scribbled on the note pad all he could remember about the re-corded message.

He had written on the pad: "You have what they want, Steven. Use it to your advantage. Estate in California. British Concorde." The word Concorde was the only word on the pad which he had underlined. And for a while he pondered the meaning of the word.

Among other things, he thought, the word Concorde meant: the capital of New Hampshire; it meant agreement or harmony; it meant a large, dark-blue grape. But what did either of those things have to do with the location of the disk?

"You 'have' what they want," Gregory recalled the statement his uncle had made. Which meant that Gregory *had* the disk in his possession, *now*, he concluded.

Gregory remembered the words that the man, who had sat at the table before him in that restaurant, said just before Gregory shot him: "We want the disk that your uncle sent to you."

Uncle Max was a very clever man, Gregory thought. Perhaps he sent the disk camouflaged. But the only thing that his uncle had sent to him recently was a bottle of wine. Could the disk have been packed in the box along with the bottle of wine? Of course not,

Gregory thought. The only thing in that box was a bottle of wine with thick sponge-like packing to protect the bottle during shipment. There was no disk.

But wait a minute, Gregory thought. Concorde—a large dark blue grape. Was his uncle hinting or suggesting wine? Could the bottle of wine have something to do with the *location* of the disk?

On the morning of their tenth wedding anniversary, after receiving the bottle of wine from his uncle, Gregory's wife had suggested that they call Uncle Max and thank him for the anniversary gift, and so they did. After his wife had said her hello and her thanks, Gregory took the receiver.

"Hey, Uncle Max, you remembered," said Gregory.

"Of course," Max had said on the other end of the wire. "Did you think I'd forget? I wanted to send you something very special."

"It 'is' special. And just to show you how special it is, we're not going to open it until you get here and start your vacation. Freda insists that we wait for you."

"Oh, well, how nice? Oh, and Steven, this particular bottle of wine is the best that my California winery has to offer. It was made with some very 'special ingredients.' It is literally a 'treasure *map*.' A map that could lead to something *enormous*."

At the time of the telephone conversation, they had both chuckled. Gregory had not given it a second thought, but now he did. Was his uncle suggesting or hinting that a map or information of some kind was stored in the bottle of wine that could lead to the 'exact location' of the disk?

On the note pad in front of him, Gregory wrote: concord + vineyard= wine—the bottle of wine received from Uncle Max. "Special ingredients." "Treasure map." "A map that could lead to something enormous."

"Damn it!" Gregory shouted. "That's it!"

It has to be, he thought. The location of the disk was spelled out on some map or information note that was inside the bottle of wine that his uncle had sent to him.

Gregory paced about the living room in the apartment with a new surge of hope. His eyelids no longer felt heavy. He was now wide awake. He hoped that Hilderbrant would soon call so that he could tell him how he thought they could locate the disk.

Chapter 9

CARL HILDERBRANT CONTACTED FBI inspector Anthony Miller, shortly after ten P.M. It had been nearly two hours and a half since he had sat at the table in the restaurant with Miller and told him his new demands. Hilderbrant felt that he'd given Miller enough time to contact his superiors and to convey his wishes to them.

Hilderbrant knew that Miller would be at his office because in the past, whenever things would get hot, he'd never go home until he'd get things under control again. It was not unusual for him to spend the night at his office. His wife had grown accustomed to it over the years.

"It's me," said Hilderbrant when Miller finally answered the phone. "I was just checking to see if your superiors are seeing things my way."

"Under the circumstances, my superiors had no choice but to see things your way."

"That's very good, Tony," said Hilderbrant with his usual very calm voice. "I knew you could convince them. I never doubted that for a moment."

"But we may have a slight problem. One hundred thousand dollars is a lot of money. It will take a few days."

"Oh, Tony," said Hilderbrant, "you are definitely disappointing me now."

"It takes time to raise that kind of money," Miller insisted.

"Don't insult me this way, Tony. You have raised twice as much in the past within *hours*. I want you to use all of your power and influence to raise the money promptly."

"I cannot perform a miracle," said Miller.

"You 'will' this time, Tony," Hilderbrant insisted.

"It takes time," Miller said firmly.

"You have until 'eight' tomorrow night to raise the money— the same deadline that you gave Gregory to come up with the disk. I will contact you later and give you the location of the trade."

Hilderbrant hung up before Miller could speak another word.

There was a knock at the door.

Hilderbrant grabbed his gun and turned off the living room light. "Who is it?" he asked.

"It's Don," said the voice on the other side of the door. "Your doorman."

"Come in," said Hilderbrant after unlocking the door.

The doorman opened the door slowly. "Mr. Harris?"

"Close the door and turn on the light," said Hilderbrant. By the time the light came on, he had put away his gun.

"Mr. Harris," said the doorman. "There are two guys downstairs showing people your picture."

Hilderbrant had told the doorman that his name was Tom Harris.

"They asked me if I had seen you," said the doorman. "I told them no."

"Describe them to me," said Hilderbrant.

"One was kind of short; dark hair; blue jacket. The other one was taller; sandy blond hair; gray jacket; dark slacks, I think. They both wore neckties. They told me that they are FBI agents."

"But you did not tell them that you'd seen me," said Hilderbrant.

"No, sir, Mr. Harris," said the young doorman. "I did exactly like you told me. I took a good look at them so that I would be able to describe them to you."

"That's good, Don," said Hilderbrant, as he reached into his front trouser pocket. He gave the doorman a hundred-dollar bill. "I want you to go back downstairs and keep your eyes open."

"Yes, sir, Mr. Harris," said the doorman. "Don't worry about nothing." He left the room and closed the door.

Hilderbrant had paid the doorman a one hundred-dollar bill earlier that day, just to give him the information that he'd just received. And now Hilderbrant was sure that Anthony Miller had given the order to kill him.

Hilderbrant new how persistent the Feds could be, so he decided that it was time for him to vacate the premises. It was only a matter of time, he thought, before they'd close in on him.

~~~~

Hilderbrant got off the elevator on the first floor. The lobby was quite active that night because of the big party which had just ended in the ballroom. It had been a formal event—an evening gown dinner jacket affair—which made it much easier for Hilderbrant to spot the less formally dressed FBI agents. As he moved toward the front entrance of the hotel, Hilderbrant noticed a man who fitted the description of one of the FBI agents. The man was short with dark hair and he was wearing a blue jacket, just as the doorman had described him.

Hilderbrant decided to pick the two FBI agents off with his gun and then leave the building. He saw the short one, but he did not see the tall one with the blond hair and gray jacket.

The short FBI agent stood at the hotel entrance with his arms folded. Hilderbrant was standing near the wall amid a group of individuals who had recently left the ballroom. The unconscionable killer was growing impatient and decided to make his move. He slowly walked toward the hotel entrance and noticed that the FBI agent had lit up a cigarette.

Hilderbrant stopped at the glass door and looked outside at the FBI agent. Then Hilderbrant pulled out his thirty-eight revolver with the silencer, placed the point of the gun against the glass door, and pulled the trigger.

The FBI agent on the other side of the glass door fell with a fatal bullet wound to the head. Hilderbrant was standing about twelve feet from the corpse. He was about to open the door and leave the building when the other FBI agent with the blond hair rushed over to the dead agent. He had come from the area near the street, and was talking into his radio.

Hilderbrant decided not to leave the hotel through the front entrance, for he had no idea how many FBI agents were out there waiting for him.

The FBI agent with the radio, who was kneeling over his dead partner, looked up at the glass door and saw Hilderbrant staring down at him. He drew his gun and fired once at Hilderbrant, missing him by only inches, but shattered the glass door. Hilderbrant returned fire with one shot, and then moved quickly from the entrance. He mixed with the startled crowd as four FBI agents entered the building with guns drawn.

"Hold it!" Shouted one of the agents. "FBI!"

Hilderbrant turned and fired twice. One of the shots hit an agent in the chest. The second shot hit a woman in the arm. Everyone in the immediate area scattered and or dropped to the floor to avoid the gunfire.

Hilderbrant moved swiftly to the elevator and shielded himself with a young woman as he waited for the elevator doors to open. The FBI agents looked on helplessly with guns drawn and pointed at Hilderbrant.

"Please don't kill me," the woman was crying as Hilderbrant gripped the hair on her head tightly, shifting her body about to shield his own.

"Please!" She continued with pain. "You're hurting me!"

The elevator doors opened and Hilderbrant stepped inside with the woman. Then when the doors started to close, he pushed the woman out of the elevator and fired once more at the agents, just before the elevator doors closed.

The hotel lobby was filled with chaos; with screams and shock, as the FBI agents stood before the elevator doors, watching the numbers light up, trying to determine on which floor Hilderbrant would exit.

Hilderbrant was alone in the elevator as it travelled up to the fifth floor. When the elevator stopped, the doors opened and Hilderbrant swiftly stepped off and rushed down the hall to his hotel room. He was holding his gun downward.

He entered his hotel room and slammed the door shut. There was no time to lose. He removed the silencer and holstered his gun. On the dresser was an eighteen-inch automatic weapon. Hilderbrant grabbed the gun and placed several clips for that gun in his coat pockets, and then he left the room.

~~~~

Downstairs in the hotel lobby, Special Agent Crumwell had arrived. He had just stepped over the corpse of the FBI agent lying in a puddle of blood at the entrance of the hotel. The shattered glass made a crackling gritty sound as the bottom of Crumwell's shoes made contact with it.

"Somebody, please get a doctor!" Shouted the man who knelt over the woman with the arm wound.

Crumwell was approached quickly by another agent with a radio.

"It's Hilderbrant," said the other agent. "We've got him cornered on the fifth floor. I'm in contact with Baxter now."

Crumwell took the radio from the agent's hand and spoke into it. "Baxter," he said. "This is Crumwell. What's the situation up there?"

Before Agent Baxter could respond, Crumwell heard the sounds of automatic weapons being fired on the other end of the radio.

"Damn," said Crumwell. Then he looked at the agent who stood before him. "Cover every exit! Get some men on it fast! I'm going up."

Taking the elevator up to the fifth floor would be risky, so Crumwell headed for the stairs with his gun drawn. He climbed to the fifth floor with difficulty. He was badly out of shape. As he moved with increased caution, he inhaled and exhaled deeply, trying to catch his breath.

The hallway was deserted. Crumwell walked past a room with an open door. It was Hilderbrant's room. Crumwell continued down the hall to the elevator where he found three FBI agents. They were all dead. The walls had been riddled with bullets fired from automatic weapons. The gun battle had been fierce with Hilderbrant emerging the victor. And he had escaped.

Later, special agent Crumwell learned that Hilderbrant had taken the freight elevator to the first floor and had escaped through the kitchen where he exited the hotel, after he'd threatened several cooks and other employees with death if they'd dare get in his way.

~~~~

The next day at twelve noon, FBI Inspector Anthony Miller sat alone at a table in his favorite restaurant. He was having lunch at the same table where nearly seventeen hours ago he'd sat with Carl Hilderbrant.

Miller had been informed about the hotel shoot-out with Hilderbrant on the previous evening and was greatly disappointed that Hilderbrant had not been killed. But he felt confident that his men would eventually get the job done. Steven Gregory was the only man on whom Miller wanted to focus one hundred percent of his attention.

"Hi, Tony," said the man who stood behind Miller, touching the inspector's shoulder lightly.

Miller turned his head in the direction of the voice and looked up. The man who was touching his shoulder was Carl Hilderbrant.

Hilderbrant gave Miller's shoulder a friendly pat, and then he moved to the opposite side of the table and sat facing the FBI inspector.

Miller had suddenly lost his appetite for lunch. He would have reached for his gun to kill Hilderbrant right there, but he was not wearing one. He swallowed with difficulty as fear became evident on his face, as his pulse began to race.

"You disappoint me, Tony," said Hilderbrant calmly. "You should not have sent your men after me last night."

Miller tried to get up from the table but Hilderbrant slapped the table quickly and said, "Don't get up on my account, Tony."

Miller wanted to run but he knew that Hilderbrant was a man who was always armed with a gun and that if he really wanted him dead, he'd shoot him in the back.

"Don't be afraid, Tony," said Hilderbrant. "I'm not here to harm you. I still need you to make this deal work."

Miller felt a faint shimmer of hope and thought that perhaps he would not die.

"I want you to call your men off," said Hilderbrant. "I want to start fresh. But this time, there will be no tricks."

Miller sat silently, giving his full attention to Hilderbrant.

"Of course, you realize that the money 'will' be dropped on schedule tonight," said Hilderbrant. "I Trust you did not become overconfident that I would be killed, therefore ending your efforts to raise the money that we had both agreed on."

Miller bowed his head slightly as if to suggest with guilt that he had indeed stopped trying to raise the money.

"But if you 'were' stupid enough to do something as dumb as that," Hilderbrant continued, "then that means that you—because of your complacency—will now have to double your efforts to meet the eight o'clock deadline. You 'must' have the money by eight o'clock tonight. I will contact your office tonight at seven. You will tell me that you have the money. And then I will tell you where to drop the money. It will be an even exchange—the money for the disk.

Miller sighed, and then added, "I will have the money for you tonight."

Hilderbrant nodded his approval. "That's good, Tony," he said. "That's what I wanted to hear. Forgive me for interrupting your lunch, but I just felt that I had to meet with you face to face to convey my feelings."

Miller hated Hilderbrant's placidness with a passion. The unconscionable killer always seemed to have the winning card.

"I will leave you, now," said Hilderbrant, "so that you might finish your lunch." He rose from the table and started to leave, but then he stopped suddenly. "Oh, Tony" he said. "I almost forgot. I *really* need to set an example for your people. You remember when I said I still need you?"

"Yes," said Miller.

"Well, strike that," said Hilderbrant. "I lied. I think I'll do business with your agent Crumwell."

Hilderbrant drew his gun with a silencer attached to it. He pointed the gun at Miller and fired five shots rapidly into his body, as several individuals at the adjacent tables looked on with shock. Expressionless, Hilderbrant holstered his gun and left the restaurant.

Outside, parked near the curb, was Hilderbrant's taxi cab. Hilderbrant got into the back seat of the cab and said to the driver, "Okay, let's go." When the driver pulled out into the traffic, Hilderbrant gave the driver a one hundred-dollar bill. It had been the third bill he'd given to the driver since he flagged the cab down nearly two hours ago.

"You can become a rich man today," Hilderbrant said to the cab driver. "All you have to do is drive and forget my face."

The driver's eyes opened widely at the sight of the money. "Yes, sir" he said, "You've got it."

Hilderbrant leaned back against the seat and sighed faintly, as he looked thoughtfully, straight ahead through the windshield.

Chapter 10

IT WAS FEBRUARY 7. The physical violence had all started four days ago with the explosion of a bomb which nearly killed his wife. Steven Gregory had slept very little on the previous night and he cursed Hilderbrant for not contacting him as he had said he would.

It was about one P.M. And time was running out for Gregory. He had only seven hours left to produce the disk which the FBI wanted, or his wife would die—those were the options spelled out by Carl Hilderbrant. But in order to produce the disk, Gregory would have to get back to his home and find the bottle of wine that his Uncle Max had sent to him. It was a long shot for sure, he thought. But he had to try.

The apartment was so deathly quiet that Gregory could not take it any longer. It was just too quiet for him. He moved to the television set in the living room and turned it on. A soap opera was on the tube, his wife's favorite. It was Friday and Gregory knew they would build the show to a cliff hanger which would hold the audience interest until Monday's show.

For nearly ten minutes, Gregory listened to the voices of the soap opera characters on TV, but he really didn't comprehend, for his thoughts were dominated only by the memories of his wife. The fact that he had not had breakfast and his stomach was growling was of minor importance.

Suddenly, the soap opera was interrupted by a special news bulletin.

"We will now go live to the scene of the crime," said the voice on the television.

Gregory's attention was drawn to the television screen as the female news reporter was standing at the entrance of the Yorkshire Restaurant.

". . . where only moments ago," said the reporter, "the local FBI Inspector Anthony Miller was shot down in cold blood while having lunch. Witnesses say a lone gunman entered the restaurant and sat for a short while at the inspector's table. The two men talked briefly; then suddenly, without warning, the unidentified man pulled out a gun and shot the inspector five times in the chest."

Gregory frowned as he moved closer to the television set. He remembered the name Anthony Miller. He was the man who was the key to getting his wife back—according to Hilderbrant.

"Witnesses described the gunman as being tall and slender, in his early thirties," the reporter continued.

The telephone rang and Gregory picked up the receiver quickly before it could ring again.

"Hello," he said.

"It's me—Hilderbrant," said the voice on the other end of the wire.

"Where the hell have you been?" said Gregory. "Why didn't you call?" He looked at the television screen. "We've got a problem."

"What problem?" asked Hilderbrant.

"I'm looking at a special news report on TV. The man who you said could lead me to my wife has just been shot and killed in a restaurant."

"There's nothing to worry about," said Hilderbrant. "Do you know where the disk is?"

There was a pause, and then Gregory said. "I think I do, yes. But who will we deal with now? The key man is dead."

"No problem. We will deal with the second man in control. His name is Crumwell. Everything will work out okay. Miller 'had' to die."

"What do you mean he *had* to die," said Gregory, recalling the eyewitnesses' description on TV of the gunman who had shot Miller: tall, slender, and early thirties. "My God," Gregory continued. "You sonofabitch—it was you. You killed Miller. What happened to that mutual respect that you were telling me you two had for each other?"

"No need to get upset, Gregory."

"My wife could die because of you," Gregory growled.

"Just tell me where the disk is."

"Forget it! I'll make the deal with Crumwell myself."

"That's stupid, Gregory. I know how to deal with these people. You're out of your league. You're dealing with pros."

"I'll take my chances," said Gregory. Then he hung up with a slam!

"Damn!" Gregory continued.

He had to move fast.

Gregory sighed deeply and thought for a moment. He could no longer trust Hilderbrant, so now he had to battle the FBI alone. He decided to first obtain the disk, and then he would contact the FBI man whose name was Crumwell. He had no time to lose.

Gregory went to Hilderbrant's bedroom and grabbed the briefcase from the bed, which contained the twenty thousand dollars. He opened it and took a handful of money. He didn't count it. He just stuffed it into the pocket of his jacket. He would need the money, he thought, so that he could move around more freely— for transportation or to pay for a favor which could save his life. Money talks when you're on the streets. He knew that from experience.

Next, he needed a weapon—some type of protection. He could conceal neither the high-powered rifle nor the eighteen inch automatic weapon which were both lying on the bed near the briefcase. He needed something smaller, and thanks to Hilderbrant, there was no problem. Gregory noticed an automatic pistol on the top of the dresser.

He grabbed up the pistol and then put three clips for that weapon into his pocket. Now he was set. He was ready.

He went to the living room. The television set was still on and the soap opera was back on the screen. He moved apprehensively to the door, hesitated for a moment, and then left the apartment.

Gregory went down the hall to the elevator and stepped inside. He took the elevator down to the parking area below the building. He had decided against leaving the building through the front entrance. The back way would be safer for him, he thought. Since the day of the bomb explosion which nearly killed his wife, Gregory had become paranoid, associating any front entrance with overexposure.

But this time, his caution did not pay off. Only seconds after he'd reached the parking area, a man of medium build suddenly came up from behind him and pointed a gun at Gregory's back.

"Don't move," said the man with the gun. "I'll waste you right here if you try anything funny." He pressed the gun against Gregory's back. "You got that?"

"I understand" said Gregory, raising his hands slightly.

"Put your hands down," the man growled. "This ain't a fuckin' stickup. You want people to see you with your hands up in the air? Don't make us look so obvious. Move over there to the brown car."

Gregory lowered his hands as the man moved closer to him, nudging him in the back, as if to conceal the gun or at least appear less obvious.

They moved to the brown car.

"Get in the car," said the man with the gun.

Gregory was about to get into the back seat.

"Not the back seat," the man said. "Get in the front seat. C'mon."

Gregory got into the car and sat opposite the steering wheel as the man with the gun got into the back seat and sat directly behind him.

"Put your hands on top of the dashboard," said the man, "and don't move."

Gregory put his hands on the dashboard as requested and looked down at his waistband. He saw the bulging butt of the gun which was concealed underneath the jacket which he wore. The man who now held a gun on him was probably an amateur, Gregory thought. The man did not even search him to see if he were carrying a gun.

"Hilderbrant told me that you might try to leave the building this way," said the man. "He knows you like a book."

Gregory sighed. Hilderbrant could not be trusted, he thought, as he made note of the smell of the car. The elegant Ford was a new car. At least, it smelled like it was new.

The man who held the gun on Gregory coughed suddenly. His eyes were watery and he could use a shave. He was clearly a drug addict. "I was supposed to follow you and report back to Hilderbrant with your location. But I struck a better deal. So you just sit tight. They will be here shortly."

"Who will be here shortly?" Gregory asked.

"You just don't talk, damn it. That asshole Hilderbrant thinks that he can buy my services for a lousy one hundred dollars. You're hot property, man. Everybody wants you"

"Look," said Gregory. "I can make you a better deal. I've got money—lots of it. There's nearly twenty thousand dollars in a briefcase upstairs in Hilderbrant's apartment."

"Shut up!" the man shouted. "You can't buy me with money."

Gregory had heard the sound of paper being unfolded; the crumpling sound of a bag, perhaps, he thought. The sounds were coming from the back seat of the car. Then he heard the man sniff suddenly, once again. He thought perhaps the man had a cold. But he was wrong. Gregory turned his head slightly, and from the corner of his eye, he glanced at the man in the back seat.

On the man's upper lip and nose was a white powdered substance which resembled cocaine. In fact, Gregory thought, it 'was' cocaine. The man had been snorting the illicit powdered substance with the tiny straw which he held in his hand. The man quickly grabbed up his gun, which he had momentarily placed on the seat, and pointed it at Gregory's head.

"Turn around!" He growled.

Gregory complied.

"Those CIA boys should be here any minute now."

CIA? Gregory thought.

"Now, those guys know how to deal," the man continued. "Those CIA boys—you know what I'm going to get in exchange for you?" He smiled maniacally. "I'm going to get some pure white cocaine."

That's it, thought Gregory. It's the CIA hit squad that Hilderbrant was speaking about a while back.

"Listen to me," said Gregory. "Those CIA guys that you're talking about are going to kill both of us. I know how they operate."

"No," the man insisted. "I know these guys. I've worked with them before. Like a few nights ago, they couldn't make it in time. They say blast whoever I see at that payphone on the corner of Royal and Clayborn. We lit that phone booth up! I killed that motherfucker!"

As Gregory turned his head slightly, trying to see the man's exact location, he now realized that this was the same person who had tried to kill him at that pay phone a few nights ago.

"I'd like to see Hilderbrant's face when he finds out that he's lost you." The man laughed and then sniffed at the cocaine again.

Gregory sat very still and silently for nearly two minutes trying to build enough courage to reach for the gun under his waistband. He turned his head slightly, trying to see the exact location of the man in the back seat, who then suddenly pressed his gun against the back of Gregory's neck.

"Don't keep pressing your luck with me, sonofabitch," said the man. "I'm warning you. Don't turn your head again."

"Alright, alright!" Gregory said, raising his hands high as he felt the coldness of the gun against his neck.

"Put your hands back on the dash!"

"Okay, okay," said Gregory, with a cautious placatory voice. "Just don't panic. I want to work with you."

"I don't panic!" The man growled.

"Fine," said Gregory. "Okay. Whatever you say." He had returned his hands to the dashboard.

Gregory felt the pressure of the gun against his neck being reduced. The man with the gun suddenly turned his head to the right and noticed a car approaching them. "Good," he said. "Here they come now."

Gregory panicked. His pulse began to race. He had to make a move. It was now or never. The men who were approaching them in the car would certainly kill him. They were with the CIA hit squad sent to murder him.

Gregory reached quickly for the automatic pistol under his jacket. He might die making the sudden move, but Gregory was convinced that now was the time. He gritted his teeth and then yelled, as if to frighten away the bullet which he knew he could not stop.

He turned quickly as he yelled and fired at the man behind him. Before he released the trigger, he had fired four shots. The first bullet jerked the man's head back and splattered blood on the back of the seat. The second bullet struck the back of the seat and the last two shattered the rear window.

Gregory sat unsteady as he stared at the corpse. And the roar of a car's engine and the sound of tires screeching to an abrupt halt startled him.

He lowered his head just in time. The two men in the car which had just pulled up suddenly opened fire with machine guns. As bits and pieces of shattered glass dropped all around him, Gregory tried to squeeze himself between the steering wheel and the accelerator.

The car key was in the ignition. When the shooting stopped, Gregory reached for the key and started the engine. He shifted the car to reverse, then he pressed his hand down on the accelerator and the car sped off backward and crashed into the side of a parked car. He shifted to "drive" and the shooting started again briefly.

Gregory raised his gun and fired rapidly at the men who were firing at him. Then he turned the wheel to the right and sat upright. He sped off suddenly and almost hit one of the two gunmen and then scraped the side of their car. And once again the two men fired at Gregory. Gregory lowered his head as he started to exit the parking area.

He blindly drove the car out into the traffic and crashed into the side of a yellow cab. He was shaken by the crash but no one was injured. He managed to slowly raise himself from the seat. He was a bit dazed but quickly realized that he had to run for his life.

He got out of the car and in the distance, he could see the two armed men running toward him with their guns drawn.

Because of the heavy afternoon traffic, automobiles were lined up for nearly a block, as the traffic light changed to red. Gregory started to run in the direction of the idle traffic on that one-way street, with his gun in his hand. There were two lanes of traffic and Gregory was in the middle of the street, with cars on either side of him.

Ahead, near the traffic light, was a Greyhound bus. The light changed to green and the automobile traffic started to move slowly forward. One of the CIA men chasing Gregory suddenly opened fire. The bullets from his automatic weapon riddled adjacent cars indiscriminately, as Gregory took cover behind one car after another.

When he thought the moment was right, Gregory rose from behind a car and fired twice at the gunman. One of Gregory's shots hit the man. Gregory saw him fall to the pavement but he did not know he had killed him.

A car had stalled in front of the Greyhound bus ahead, slowing the traffic even more. The bus driver started to pull around the stalled car as Gregory began to run. Gregory considered stopping the bus and using it as an escape vehicle. The second CIA man was closing in on him.

Gregory caught up with the bus just as it pulled around the stalled car and desperately tried to stop it by striking the side of it just below the driver's window. He struck the bus several times with his hand as he ran alongside it, shouting at the driver.

When the bus driver reduced his speed, Gregory was able to step in front of the bus. He pointed his gun at the driver through the windshield. "Stop the bus!" he shouted. "Stop the bus!"

The driver complied.

"Now, open the door," Gregory shouted. "Open the door now!"

The bus driver suddenly raised his hands and nervously shook his head from side to side as if to suggest that he did not know what Gregory was saying.

While pointing the gun at the bus driver, Gregory pointed to his lips with a finger of his left hand. "Read my lips," he shouted. "Open the door or I will blow your damned head off."

Gregory was now standing in front of the bus holding the gun with both hands and ready to fire into the windshield.

The bus driver quickly opened the door and Gregory moved to the side of the bus and hopped inside. Gregory instructed the driver to close the door.

"Okay, let's get out of here!" Gregory shouted.

And the driver accelerated.

Gregory looked into the faces of a busload of frightened people.

"Oh, God," said one woman. "Please don't let him kill us."

A man suddenly attempted to get out of his seat. Gregory pointed his gun at the passengers on the bus.

"Nobody moves!" he shouted.

A woman screamed and the passengers lowered their heads.

"Everyone listen to me," Gregory continued. "Put your hands on the back of the seat in front of you. I want to see your hands. C'mon! Let's do it!"

Everyone complied with Gregory's request.

"I don't want to hurt anyone," he said. "Where are you headed?" Gregory asked the driver.

"We're headed for Oakland," he answered.

"Okay," said Gregory. "Stay on course. And please do as I say. I don't want anyone to get hurt."

"Yes, sir," said the driver.

Gregory then directed his attention to the passengers on the bus. He glanced at them with his gun pointed upward. He truly hated what he'd done, but he had to escape from those CIA hit men. He prayed to God that no one on that bus would try to rush him and try to take the gun from him, for he really did not know how he would react. They were all innocent people, he thought. The victims of circumstance, just as he was. And he hated it.

As the bus moved onward, Gregory thought of the drug addict who had held a gun on him in the parking area below the apartment building where he had spent the previous night. He had shot and killed the drug addict. He frowned at the thought. He had watched as the man's head exploded.

"Is this the way I must live now?" He thought. "Must I kill to survive? When will it all end?"

As the bus travelled across the Golden Gate Bridge, Gregory considered the valuable time that he was losing. He was moving further and further away from his home. The delay could cause him to lose his wife.

~~~~

At the local FBI Office downtown, Special Agent Crumwell had received a call from Washington, D.C., in response to the death of FBI inspector Anthony Miller.

Only moments later, as he sat alone in Miller's office, the telephone rang again.

"Crumwell here," he said after he snatched up the receiver and placed it to his ear.

"Listen to me carefully," said the voice on the other end of the wire. "This is Hilderbrant. Inspector Miller was a very stupid man. So now he's dead. But I would very much like to do business with you, Mr. Crumwell."

"I'm listening," said Crumwell.

"I have Steven Gregory hidden away in a safe place. You *can't* get to him. It must be understood that I now represent Mr. Gregory. This means that you will do business with me."

"I understand," said Crumwell.

"Good. Now here are my demands: First, I want you to pull back your men. I want some breathing space. I don't like the idea of being followed. Second, you 'will' have the one hundred thousand dollars which I've requested in exchange for the disk which you 'all' want so badly. I'm sure Miller has mentioned the money to you."

"He did," Crumwell said, "and we 'will' have the money by 8 o'clock"

"That's very good, Mr. Crumwell. You sound like you are a very smart man, but in an attempt to make certain that you don't run astray as did Inspector Miller—God rest his soul—I think that I should demonstrate to you my intense desire to see to it that we have no further foul-ups. Would you please step over to your window and take a look at the car parked in front of your building? And bring your phone with you."

Crumwell was a bit hesitant, but then he moved to the window. "Okay, I'm at the window," said Crumwell.

"There's a black car parked near the curb," Hilderbrant continued. "Two FBI agents are inside."

Suddenly there was an explosion. The car which was occupied by the two FBI agents went up in flames. Crumwell watched with his mouth agape, as one of the bodies twirled out from the car.

"Yes, I did that," said Hilderbrant, on the other end of the wire. "I'm in a phone booth, holding in my hand the detonator which caused the explosion. I'm very serious, Mr. Crumwell. We will exchange the disk for the money. Do you understand me, Mr. Crumwell?"

Crumwell paused briefly and then he said with a somber voice "I understand."

"And as a bonus to you," Hilderbrant concluded, "I will do what I was originally hired to do. After I get the disk for you I will personally kill Steven Gregory."

Chapter 11

MOST OF THE passengers on the Greyhound bus were still quite tense when they reached Oakland. Gregory had kept a watchful eye on them, keeping the gun in his hand visible, by raising it high periodically so that everyone could see it and understand that he was in full control of the situation. Hopefully, Gregory thought, the gun would deter anyone who was considering being a hero.

As the bus travelled onward, Gregory became more and more uneasy. One of the two CIA men who were after him was alive and well. Gregory felt certain that the gunman had seen him get onto the bus; by now, he had told his affiliates and superiors. Perhaps the FBI had been informed too, since the two agencies were working together to some degree. They were looking for the bus at that very moment, Gregory considered. He had to get off the bus very soon.

Gregory turned to the bus driver and said, "Okay, here's where I get off. Stop the bus."

The driver slowly reduced the speed of the bus until it came to a smooth stop.

"As soon as I get off this bus," Gregory said to the driver, "I want you to get the hell out of here! Don't stop and don't look back."

"Yes, sir, Mr." said the driver. "Don't worry. I'll do exactly what you say." He opened the door.

Gregory got off the bus and quickly put his gun under his waistband, concealed by the jacket that he wore. He watched as the bus pulled off promptly.

As he stood on the side of the street in front of a fast food restaurant, Gregory silently debated his next move. He needed transportation badly, but he didn't want to force his way into someone's car and demand transportation at gunpoint. From the bus, he had noticed a used car lot a couple of blocks back. He had money now. He would go there to buy a car to get back to San Francisco.

He shoved his hands into the pockets of his jacket and started for the used car lot. He jogged for a while, then walked, then jogged until he reached the car lot. The large sign above the small building read: Floyd's Used Cars and Trucks.

Gregory noticed a car salesman in the lot, trying to make a sale to a young couple. Though they were a good distance away, Gregory could hear bits and pieces of the conversation. The salesman was doing most of the talking.

Gregory had his eyes focused on an older model Ford. It was a two-door type. Blue. On the windshield of the car, the price was spelled out with white numbers: three thousand dollars. Gregory reached into the right pocket of his jacket and pulled out a handful of one hundred dollar bills. He counted three thousand dollars and returned the remainder to his pocket. He had more than enough money to buy the car.

"Friendly Floyd is my name," said the man who had approached Gregory from behind. "Selling cars is my game. Why don't you let me put you into this light blue Chevy gem. We finance—"

"I'll take it!" Gregory interrupted. He reached for the man's hand and gripped it firmly. Then he slapped the money down in the salesman's hand and said. "Three thousand dollars. I'm in a hurry. Would you please get me the keys?"

"Good God, yes, partner", said the obese salesman with a receding hairline, and freckled scalp. "C'mon in and let me write you up."

"There's no time for that," Gregory insisted. "I'm late for an important job interview. So either you rush inside and get me the keys or you can return my money."

The salesman raised the hand with the money in it very high and away from Gregory, as if to keep him from grabbing for it and said, "I'm getting your keys 'now', sir."

Gregory watched as the large salesman turned quickly, kissed the money, and then rushed into the building for the car keys. Gregory had never seen a man that large move so quickly.

Gregory opened the door of the blue Ford and sat behind the wheel. Within a few moments the salesman had returned with the keys.

"It's all yours," said the salesman as he gave the keys to Gregory. "We can do the paperwork later. Just swing by later today. I'll be here."

Gregory slipped the key into the ignition and tried to start the car, but it would not start.

"Haven't I seen you somewhere before?" asked the salesman.

"No, you have not!" Gregory snapped. "And this damned car won't start!"

"Well, sir," the salesman explained. "It's been sitting on the lot for a couple of days. Please try again. Press down on the accelerator and—"

Gregory tried again and the engine started up. He made it roar and thick black smoke came out of the exhaust pipe.

"My cars are guaranteed," said the salesman. "If you have any problems with this baby, you bring it right back and we will take care of it."

Gregory closed the car door and pulled out of the car lot. As he turned onto the street, the hubcap on the left rear tire fell off. After he was about four blocks from the used car lot, Gregory noticed that the car that he was driving was almost out of gas. He would have to find a gas station very soon or he would be walking again. Getting gas shouldn't be a problem, he thought. There was a gas station at the corner of almost every ninth street he approached.

He didn't want to take any chances. He pulled into the next gas station ahead on the left. All of the self-service pumps were in use, so he parked his car at a full service pump where the gasoline was a bit higher in price.

"What can I do for you today?" Said the gas station attendant as he approached the car.

"Fill it up," said Gregory.

"How about under the hood?" the attendant asked.

"It's fine," Gregory insisted. "Just gas, please. I'm in a hurry."

The attendant moved promptly to the gasoline pump, removed the nozzle and began to fill the tank of the blue Ford.

Gregory sat silently behind the wheel, glancing back periodically through the rearview mirror, as the attendant filled the gas tank. But suddenly, Gregory noticed a police car pulled up slowly behind his car. He became uneasy and reached for his gun, but did not pull it from under his waistband.

The policeman got out of his car and joined the attendant at the rear of Gregory's car. With his hands gripping the gun under his jacket, Gregory got out of his car and headed for the men's room on the left side of the gas station near the rear. He walked slowly and with caution, hoping that the police officer would not recognize him. He had decided that if the police officer were to confront him, Gregory would turn his gun on the officer and fire.

Fortunately, he did not have to take drastic measures. He entered the tiny men's room and slammed the door shut. With his back against the door, Gregory closed his eyes and sighed. He felt safe for the moment. He opened the door slightly and looked in the direction of the police officer and the gas station attendant. He could see them both very clearly. They were talking as though they knew each other. They were both laughing about something.

Gregory closed the door to the men's room. The police officer was not interested in the blue Ford that he had just bought, and did not seemed to be suspicious of Gregory either. The officer had only pulled up to talk to the gas station attendant who was perhaps his friend. But Gregory would not take any chances. He remained in the men's room for nearly ten minutes. He would not come out until the police officer got back into his patrol car and drove away.

He was relieved to get out of that men's room where the air was stale and unpleasant. He went inside of the main section of the gas station. Standing behind the cash register was a second attendant.

"What can I do for you?" The attendant asked.

"You're not the one," said Gregory. "Where's the other guy who filled my tank?"

"You mean Jeff? There he is behind you. He's coming in right now."

"So, 'there' you are," said the attendant, who had been talking to the police officer. "I was wondering where you ran off to." He was smiling faintly.

"How much do I owe you?" Gregory asked.

"That will be eighteen-fifty," the man said.

Gregory reached into his pocket and peeled off a hundred-dollar bill. He slapped it down near the register. "Here," he said. "Keep the change"

Gregory then rushed out to his car and sped off into the street.

The attendant grabbed the hundred-dollar bill and smiled at his eighty-one dollar and fifty cent tip.

~~~~

Later that evening, at five before seven, Gregory was only four blocks away from his home when the blue Ford broke down. The car's engine was overheated. As if it were coming from a hot tea kettle, steam began to escape from the car's radiator. Gregory had pushed the car too hard.

In spite of Gregory's futile effort to keep the car moving, the car stopped in the middle of the street. He had pressed the accelerator all the way down to the floor, but the car slowly came to a halt.

"C'mon, damn it!" Gregory growled.

He turned the key in the ignition and tried to restart the car in spite of steam escaping from under the hood. When he realized that the car would not start, he leaned his head forward against the steering wheel.

"I don't believe this sonofabitch!" He shouted. He was disgusted. He had pushed the old car too hard. It just had to happen, he reasoned, after traveling a number of miles at an excessive rate of speed.

He got out of the car and slammed the door shut, then kicked the door twice in angry frustration. He moved to the front of the car and raised the hood with a jerky movement. The steam from the radiator struck his face with a force which demanded attention. He stepped back instantly slapping at the steam with both hands, as hot water and coolant escaped with great force from a ruptured radiator hose.

He was standing in the middle of the hot water which dripped from the radiator. So Gregory slammed the hood down, turned away from the car and started to run down the street. The car's headlights were still on, but it didn't matter. Time was running out for him and he knew that. His only concern now was getting to his home as quickly as his feet could get him there.

The night was a cool one. It was almost fifty-seven degrees, but Gregory did not notice. After running for nearly three long blocks as fast as his legs and feet would allow, his clothes were wet with perspiration.

He stopped running suddenly, but he did not stop moving. In spite of the fact that his lungs ached, he continued to walk as he inhaled and exhaled deeply. It was a quiet night. The streets were deserted. In fact, it was so quiet, he could hear himself breathing—deep heavy breathing—as he continued onward; and the footsteps, as the shoes on his feet made contact with the pavement.

Calling on the last bit of strength left in his body, Gregory began to run again. But this time he ran without graceful movement. He lacked the coordination of a fresh runner. He ran and ran until finally, in the distance, he could see his home.

But then he stopped abruptly. Paranoia began to take over again. What if his house was being watched, he thought. He would have to approach with caution for sure, but it was a chance he had to take. He could not turn back now. It was too late and he had no alternative. He thought of his wife and dismissed the possibility of a confrontation with his adversaries.

There were no unfamiliar cars in the immediate area which would suggest to Gregory that a surveillance team was near and keeping a watchful eye on his home. No strange vans or trucks. Everything seemed normal.

With the exception of the sound of a dog barking in the distance, all was quiet in the neighborhood.

Gregory shoved his hands into the pockets of the jacket which he wore and walked slowly along the sidewalk, heading for his home. He could see his home very clearly now, as he moved closer and closer. He periodically glanced backward and from side to side, to see if there were anyone following him.

And now he was only two houses away from his home, a modest two-story, just as the majority of the other homes in the neighborhood. When he reached his front lawn, he paused. Then, in a moment, he started toward the front door. All of the lights in the house were turned off.

As he approached the front door of his home, Gregory noticed something very strange. With the help of the moon, which shone brightly that night, and the adjacent street light, Gregory could see a sign posted on his door. The sign read: No Trespassing, by order of the FBI.

He frowned. He noticed that an extra lock had been attached to his door. It had been placed there by the FBI. He grabbed the doorknob and tried to unlock the door with his key, but his attempt proved fruitless. He pulled and jerked desperately at the door, but it would not open. With the bottom of his fist, he struck the door once in angry protest, and then he kicked it.

Gregory moved to the side of the house to check the windows and he found that they were all locked. All of the curtains were closed, so he could not see into the house. When he reached the rear of his house, the tall lamp post in the patio, with automatic timer, was already on. He moved promptly to the glass door which led to the kitchen. He tried to open the door by pulling and jerking, but like the front door, a new lock had been added.

"Damn it!" He growled.

He had come so far, but now he couldn't get into his own home, thanks to the FBI. It was then that he started to wonder if he could be wrong about his conclusion that the bottle of wine that his uncle had sent to him, actually contained information that would lead to the location of the disk. But Gregory refused to give up. He decided to break the glass door. He could not use his bare hands, so he looked around for something that he could charge the door with, but there was nothing.

In desperation, Gregory kicked out the lower glass panes in the door, one by one. And then he started at the wooden door frame, kicking and stomping until the door was completely ruined. Gregory's right leg was cut twice below the knee by glass, in the process. But he did not notice his injuries right away.

He bowed forward and lowered his head even more as he entered his home cautiously, underneath the jagged edges of sharp broken glass which had remained loosely hanging in the door frame. He flinched in the darkness as he cut his hand slightly on glass as he reached out for support; he almost lost his balance after stepping onto the broken glass on the kitchen floor.

Gregory ignored the cut on his hand and flicked on the kitchen light. He moved slowly and with caution to the living room. Once there, he flicked on the light and noticed a lamp and framed eight-by-ten wedding picture of his wife and himself, overturned on the floor; both of which, had fallen from an adjacent glass table. He moved slowly toward the rectangular table, knelt down and placed the gun in his hand onto the floor. With both hands, he slowly removed the picture from the floor and stared thoughtfully at it for a moment. Then he glanced about the room. Some of the furniture had been overturned and a couple of lamps were broken. It was all the result of an intense search for the computer disk.

The initial search had occurred a few days ago when Gregory and his wife had been out celebrating their tenth wedding anniversary.

Gregory suddenly moved to the bar and searched frantically for the bottle of wine which his Uncle Max had sent to him.

Where could it be?

He paused thoughtfully for a moment and recalled the morning that his wife brought the package, which contained the wine, up to their bedroom, where, while still in bed, he opened the package as his wife looked on.

That's it. The bottle of wine was still upstairs in the bedroom. It had to be there. He raced up to his bedroom and flicked on the light. The bed was the way his wife had left it. It was all made up and neat. He looked all around the room and then he noticed the bottle of wine on the dresser near the wall. His wife never got the chance to store it at the bar.

Gregory went to the dresser and picked up the bottle of wine. He stared thoughtfully at it for a moment. He sighed as he closed his eyes, hoping that he was right and that the information that would lead him to the disk was concealed inside the bottle.

He walked slowly to his bed and sat on the edge of it. He removed the seal from the top of the wine bottle, exposing the protruding *wine stopper*. It was *not* the usual cork. With a firm grip he removed the stopper from the bottle. Secured to the bottom of the stopper was a piece of wire about five inches long; and attached to the wire, and wrapped tightly and firmly in clear plastic, which had been sealed to protect it, appeared to be some type of paper rolled very tightly. It was the information or map that would lead to the location of the computer disk, Gregory thought.

Gregory stared silently at the stopper and the attachment, as his pulse rate galloped with excitement. His Uncle Max was a clever man, he thought. But now, there was no time to lose. He would have to contact that new man in charge, at the FBI office. The name was Crumwell, he recalled, as he replaced the stopper and its attachment into the bottle.

He rose from the edge of his bed and faced the bedroom doorway. To his surprise and utter shock, standing in the doorway and holding a forty-four magnum, pointed at him, was Carl Hilderbrant.

"We both deserve a glass of wine, don't you think?" said Hilderbrant.

Gregory released an audible sigh, with a feeling of defeat. He gritted his teeth and then he grimaced and swallowed with difficulty.

"How did you find me?" he said dryly. "How did you know I was here?"

"It was simple, Gregory," said Hilderbrant. "You left a trail a mile long. I returned to my apartment a short while after our telephone conversation. I didn't expect to find you there, but I found something just as good. I found the note pad that you had used to solve your uncle's word game. So, using that information, in addition to the tape recorded message that your uncle left on his telephone answering machine, I concluded that: *One*, your uncle *did* send the disk to you; *Two*, the 'information' that would lead you to the disk was here in your home somewhere; and *Three*, the location of the information that would lead to the disk had something to do with a bottle of wine that your uncle had sent you."

"How did you know the location of my home?" Gregory asked.

"When I was hired by the FBI to kill you, I had access to your file. I know as much about you as does the FBI. And believe me, Gregory, they know a lot." Hilderbrant gestured with his gun and said. "Shall we go downstairs? And bring the bottle of wine with you."

With the bottle in his hand, Gregory slowly moved to the doorway. Hilderbrant stepped to the side with his gun still pointed at Gregory and then followed him down the stairs.

"I want to thank you for breaking down the back door," Hilderbrant said. "Until you came, I just didn't know how I would get into this house."

Gregory stopped and glanced sharply at Hilderbrant.

"Yes," said Hilderbrant, "I waited outside for you to arrive. I was hiding behind the shrubs as you kicked through the door."

They continued down the stairs to the living room where they both stopped near the bar. Gregory glanced quickly at his wrist-watch. "Oh my God," he said. "Its seven fifty-eight. I've got to contact Crumwell."

"Hold it, Gregory," said Hilderbrant as Gregory attempted to move toward the phone atop the bar.

"But he'll kill my wife if I don't call!" Gregory snapped. "I have to let him know that I have the information needed to locate the disk. For God's sake, let me call."

There was a pause.

Hilderbrant said, "There's no need to call."

"What do you mean there's no need to call? You told me if I didn't hand over the disk by eight-o'clock tonight, my wife would die. So, c'mon man, let me make the call to Crumwell."

"I have to tell you, Gregory," said Hilderbrant. "Your wife is dead."

Gregory stood speechless for a moment, his mouth agape. His legs suddenly grew weak and he dropped down onto the adjacent bar stool and sat with the bottle of wine in his hand. "No," he said with a tired, sad face.

"Your wife was dead all along. Miller gave the order. So, you should thank me for killing that bastard. Everyone who was ever close to you—your family and close friends—are all dead now: your wife, your Uncle Max, your good friend Alvin Walker. All dead, Gregory."

Hilderbrant slowly moved toward Gregory. "You see, I struck a deal with Crumwell. In exchange for the disk, Crumwell will pay me one hundred thousand dollars. And so it's time now, Gregory. I want you to slowly remove the stopper from the bottle and pass the map to me."

Hilderbrant watched as Gregory placed the bottle atop the bar and removed the stopper. Gregory then reached the wine stopper and map to Hilderbrant, who moved closer to accept the prize. With the butt of his gun, Hilderbrant struck Gregory's forehead with a crushing blow, and then pulled his limp body away from the bar, to the left, allowing him to fall to the floor.

Hilderbrant placed his gun atop the bar and sighed.

"What a fucking day this has been. Don't worry Gregory, I shall return to you momentarily. I can't really kill you just yet. I have to make sure this map pans out."

Gregory was dazed. Blood was trickling down the side of his face. His body was positioned on the floor in a way that blocked Hilderbrant's view of the gun that Gregory had placed on the floor, just before he removed his wedding picture from the floor earlier.

With his back turned to Gregory, Hilderbrant was sitting at the bar having a very difficult time trying to rip open the clear plastic that was securely wrapped around the map. He gritted his teeth as he tried unsuccessfully to tare the edge of the plastic, with his fingers first, and then his teeth.

Annoyed, "Fuck!" he said. "I need a knife"

Hilderbrant glanced over his shoulder at Gregory's motionless body then rushed over to the nearby kitchen drawers and snatched open at least three of them before he finally found a knife. With the knife in hand, he went back to the bar, cut the edge of the plastic and started to remove the plastic from the map.

At that point, Gregory grabbed the gun on the floor and pulled it close. He staggered to his feet and pointed the gun at Hilderbrant, who was sitting at the bar, with his back turned to him and was attempting to unfold the map.

"So what do we have here?" Hilderbrant said, as he stared downward.

With blurred vision, Gregory slowly took aim.

Hilderbrant heard the cocking sound of the gun and he paused. Then he slowly turned his head, looking over his right shoulder, and stared at Gregory with a faint smile.

"So this is what it comes down to," Hilderbrant said.

Gregory looked at Hilderbrant's gun atop the bar, then back at Hilderbrant, who suddenly went for the gun, but was not fast enough.

Gregory fired his gun. He did not know where the bullet had hit Hilderbrant, but Gregory saw Hilderbrant's body react to the powerful force of the bullet, with a violent jerk, which sent him reeling backward to the floor, where he lay as motionless as a corpse.

Gregory lowered the gun in his hand as if it were too heavy for him to hold. He then dropped to his knees and sat on the floor in front of the bar. He was exhausted. Heartbroken. Bitter. In spite of his efforts to save his wife, she was already dead, he concluded. He had been used and manipulated just long enough to find that damned disk, he thought.

He leaned backward against the bar as he closed his eyes and frowned as blood trickled down to the corner of his left eye. He tossed the empty gun in his hand to the side and noticed that the wine stopper with the clear plastic attachment, which contained the information that could lead to the location of the disk, lying on the floor beside Hilderbrant's foot.

Gregory slowly rose from the floor, went over to the stopper and grabbed it up from the floor. He then went back to the bar and grabbed up the bottle of wine which his uncle had sent to him.

Then he moved to the stairs and sat on the fifth step from the bottom and took a sip from the bottle of wine. As he closed his eyes, he frowned.

He sniffed and then got up, reaching for the banister for support. He walked slowly up the stairs and moved to his bedroom. When he entered the bedroom, he thought of his wife. And he cursed the FBI for her death. He threw the bottle of wine angrily at the mirror on the wall just above the dresser and six drawers. Bits and pieces of the broken mirror fell on top of the dresser, amid cologne and perfume, a pink jewelry box and an eight-by-twelve picture of his wife.

Gregory walked slowly over to the dresser and reached for his wife's picture. The wine bottle had been shattered and wine was all over the top of the dresser. Some of it had started to run down the side of the dresser and drip onto the floor.

Gregory grabbed his wife's picture and stared thoughtfully at it. "My dear Freda," he said with tears in his eyes, "I'm sorry I could not protect you." He closed his eyes and embraced the picture as if it were his wife standing before him in the flesh. He sat on the edge of his bed and continued to stare at the picture. His wife's face. Her bright smile. Her long brown hair. The memories of the way she was.

~~~~

In the house next door to Gregory's house, an elderly woman stood silently at her bedroom window. She was holding her furry brown cat close to her chest as she stroked the top of the animal's head. The woman's name was Mrs. Clanton. A widow. She had moved into her new home only four days ago and was not yet very familiar with her neighbors.

Her house was the one on the corner and it was positioned in such a way that from her upstairs bedroom, she could see clearly Gregory's back yard and patio. From her bedroom window she had seen a man standing at her neighbor's back door.

Mrs. Clanton had never met her next-door neighbor. She had assumed that her new neighbor was out of town on business or vacation, since for the last four nights, not one light inside the house next door was on.

She had seen a man approach the glass door and pause for a moment. Then she saw the man kicking at the glass door.

"Oh, no" Mrs. Clanton had said as she held her cat close to her chest. "Pumpkin, look! That man is trying to break into the neighbor's house. What should we do?"

She saw the man enter the house. Then shortly afterwards, she saw a second man enter the house. But he was holding a gun in his hand. She could not see it clearly, but she was sure it was a gun. What else could it be? The man's arm was extended forward and he was holding it out in front of him, letting it lead the way as he walked with caution. The first man had turned on the bright kitchen light, so she could now see the second man a bit better.

"Oh, no, Pumpkin," she said to her cat with a low voice. "We should do something."

Moments went by and Mrs. Clanton remained at her bedroom window until she heard a single shot rang out in the house next door. She dropped her cat and stepped back from her bedroom window. With her mouth wide open, she rushed over to the phone near her bed, snatched up the receiver and dialed 911.

"Hello," she said. "Please help. I'd like to report a crime. Someone has just broken into my neighbor's house. And a gun has been fired."

Chapter 12

STEVEN GREGORY LAY flat on his back staring aimlessly at the ceiling. With the picture of his wife against his chest, he lay there in bed silently, thinking of her. "Where do I go from here?" he thought.

At that moment, he wanted nothing more than to hurt the FBI. He wanted to hurt the FBI and see it suffer, as did he, over the past few days. If he had to die trying, he wanted to see the FBI go down the tubes. But how could he, one man alone, fight such a powerful organization—the technology, the computers and the brilliant minds of the FBI. The law enforcement agency which was created to eradicate crime, Gregory thought, was now the doer of crime on a vast scale.

The contents of the disk, Gregory reasoned, would most definitely hurt the FBI. But the question was how could he expose the FBI without getting killed first. What about the news media, he considered. Those guys always like to put the heat on the government. Great idea! But the problem with that idea was living long enough to tell the story. At this point, he was now known all over the country. His picture was in post offices everywhere. The FBI made sure of that.

Gregory's name had been smeared and connected with drug dealer and big-time crime boss, Fred Ramis. And Gregory was also charged with the attempted murder of the FBI agent whom he shot at Sophie's Restaurant. Gregory reasoned that he would have a very difficult time trying to convince the media that the FBI was having an ethics problem.

So back to square one, he thought. Where do I go from here? He sat upright on the edge of the bed and placed the picture of his wife to the side. After lying there in bed for nearly fourteen minutes, he got up and went to the bathroom where he flicked on the light and stood before the mirror.

He placed the wine stopper and its attachment on the counter before him near the sink, turned the cold tap water on and then put his hands under the flow. He wet his face and he saw blood from the cut on his forehead drip into the sink. He frowned as the cut started to sting slightly.

He reached for a towel and carefully dried his face. Then suddenly, something strange happened. He thought he heard noise downstairs. It sounded like someone was trying to break down the front door. And now, for the first time, he took a closer look at the miniature map that was retrieved from the bottle of wine, which detailed the location of the disk. He memorized the contents before ripping it apart and tossing it into the toilet and giving it a flush.

~~~~

Outside, on the street, just in front of Gregory's home, six vehicles had pulled up. FBI agents with tactical gear quickly got out of those vehicles with their automatic weapons on the ready. There were twenty agents altogether. As their shoes hit the pavement, they scrambled toward the house, slamming their car doors shut.

"Surround the house!" Special Agent Crumwell shouted. And within seconds the FBI agents broke through the front door and entered the house. Some had even entered through the backdoor which Gregory had earlier broken through.

With precision, the agents quickly checked the downstairs area, and then they moved upstairs with their guns on the ready. Three agents quickly entered Gregory's bedroom and immediately saw him standing in the bathroom near the bathtub.

Gregory slammed the bathroom door shut. The agents rushed over to the door and kicked it open. Two of the agents grabbed Gregory by his shoulders and violently pushed him out of the bathroom and up against the bedroom wall. Gregory's back was turned to the agents as the right side of his face was pressed against the wall.

They searched him. A gun was pressed against the back of his head. Then he was spun around suddenly and slammed backward against the wall as the search continued. They searched his pockets, his sides, his legs.

"Where is the disk?" one agent asked.

Gregory pulled his head back angrily with a quick jerky movement, but remained silent.

Special agent Crumwell entered the room. "Alright," he said, "bring him downstairs."

"He's not talking," said one of the agents to Crumwell. "We've searched him, but he's clean. He doesn't have the disk on him."

"Downstairs," Crumwell repeated.

One agent stood on either side of Gregory and each held an arm tightly as they escorted him out of the room.

As Gregory walked down the stairs with an FBI agent on either side of him, he realized that his luck had finally run out. His living room was filled with armed FBI agents. There was no way he could escape.

At the bottom of the stairs, the agents paused suddenly. Then they took him outside. As they walked across the front lawn in the darkness, heading for the government car parked near the curb, the fatigue and the mental exhaustion started to take a toll on Gregory. He became weak and dropped to his knees.

"C'mon," said one of the agents. "Help him up. Get him to the car."

The agents helped Gregory to his feet by holding his arms firmly and then lifting him just high enough so that only his feet would drag slightly as they carried him to the car. They helped him into the back seat of the car, and then slammed the door shut.

An FBI agent was standing on either side of the car as Gregory sat on the back seat alone. As he looked back at his home, he realized that he'd never see it again.

~~~~

Inside Gregory's home, Special Agent Crumwell stood in the living room near the bar and stared downward at the blood on the carpet where earlier, Hilderbrant had laid. His body was now gone.

"Someone else was here, sir," announced an agent to Crumwell. "Whoever it was lost a lot of blood."

Crumwell followed the drops of blood through the kitchen and to the glass door which Gregory had broken. For a moment, Crumwell looked out into the darkness, and then he turned and faced the agent who had followed him.

"Tucker," he said. "I want this house sealed off!"

"Right," said Tucker.

"I want every inch of it searched," Crumwell continued. "The disk is here. What other reason would Gregory have for returning to his home?"

"Who do you think was here with Gregory?" Tucker asked.

"I don't know, but I think I have a very good idea.

"Hilderbrant?" asked Tucker.

"Exactly," said Crumwell. "It seems that Gregory got lucky. A neighbor reported to the police that she heard a shot fired. If Hilderbrant was the one who got shot, he won't get very far."

"Do you think he has the disk with him?"

"Only Gregory can tell us that," said Crumwell. "I want you to alert the police about Hilderbrant. Also, notify the hospitals. Hilderbrant might bleed to death and be picked up as a John Doe. If so, I want to know about it."

~~~~

Steven Gregory sat with his eyes closed as he leaned backward in the back seat of the car. The FBI agent who stood at the left side of the car had lit up a cigarette, while the agent on the other side of the car stood with his arms folded. Gregory heard the car door open. He opened his eyes. Crumwell was standing there looking at him.

Crumwell got into the car and sat down beside Gregory, slamming the door shut. "Steven Gregory," he said. "I'm Special Agent Crumwell with the—"

With his last bit of energy, Gregory grabbed Crumwell's throat with both hands. "I'll kill you, sonofabitch!" He growled.

In his weakened state, Gregory was no match for the more stable Crumwell who quickly struck Gregory twice in the abdomen.

Gregory released Crumwell's neck and leaned opposite Crumwell toward the door, trying to catch his breath. The FBI agent standing closest to Crumwell opened the car door to give assistance to his superior officer.

"It's Okay," said Crumwell. "Everything is under control. "Close the door."

The agent closed the door, and then Crumwell looked at Gregory and said. "I'm sorry I had to do that, Mr. Gregory. But I truly wish you would cooperate with us. You know what we want, Mr. Gregory. The disk. Tell me the location of the disk."

"Drop dead, you sick gutless bastard." Gregory was still trying to catch his breath.

"We've found bloodstains on the carpet in the living room. Who was here with you? Was it Hilderbrant?"

Gregory remained silent.

"C'mon, Gregory," Crumwell continued. "Did Hilderbrant get away with the disk?"

"If you're going to kill me, then get it over with," Gregory snapped.

"We don't want your life, Mr. Gregory," Crumwell spoke calmly. "We only want the disk."

"I don't believe you, man," said Gregory. "You've killed my wife and now you expect me to help you?"

"Your wife is not dead, Mr. Gregory. We had to transfer her to another hospital where she'd be safe."

There was a pause.

Gregory stared blankly at Crumwell for a moment, and then said, "That's a cruel joke, Crumwell. Hilderbrant told me what you people did to her just before I shot him."

"Hilderbrant lied to you, Mr. Gregory. He's very good at that."

"I thought I had killed that sonofabitch."

"You came very close to doing just that. He's lost a lot of blood for sure. Hilderbrant was hired by inspector Miller to murder you. But he didn't know the reason why you were to be murdered. You see, Hilderbrant has an international reputation for murder. So, Miller's superiors in Washington insisted that Miller hire Hilderbrant to do the job."

Gregory sighed as he listened to Crumwell.

"When Hilderbrant learned about the disk, he became greedy. He knew that the disk was very valuable. So he had to get close to you and win your confidence. His objective was to keep you alive until he'd obtained the disk. Then he'd kill you and sell the disk to the FBI—to Inspector Miller that is—for a large sum of money. One hundred thousand dollars, to be exact."

Gregory understood that he'd been used by Hilderbrant, but that didn't matter anymore. He felt certain that Crumwell was trying to use psychology to trick him just as Hilderbrant had done. Gregory was already convinced that he would never see his wife alive again, and now it was obvious, he thought, that Crumwell was trying to convince him that his wife was still alive, just so he might cooperate and turn the disk over to Crumwell.

"Trust me, Mr. Gregory," said Crumwell. "The FBI does not want to hurt you. For the past several days, we have been trying to

protect you. We learned that a CIA hit squad was sent here to obtain the disk from you at all cost and then murder you. It was they
who initially broke into your home on the night of your wedding
anniversary, while you and your wife were out celebrating. They
searched your home, but they did not find the disk."

"You're trying to tell me that the FBI had nothing to do with
the bomb which exploded at the daycare center and hospitalized
my wife?" Said Gregory.

"Exactly," Crumwell responded.

Gregory did not believe a word of what Crumwell was telling
him. "You're lying, Crumwell," Gregory growled. "The man who I
shot at Sophie's Restaurant claimed responsibility for the bomb and
the break-in of my home. He *was* an FBI agent. The news reports
on television and radio confirmed that"

"The man who you shot was a member of that CIA hit
squad," Crumwell insisted. "Inspector Miller arranged it so that
the news media would announce that *you* attempted to murder an
FBI agent, because a CIA connection would have had undesir-
able implications. He wanted to smear your name and connect
you with notorious drug dealers, so that if you were to suddenly
turn up dead, everyone would conclude that you were just another ex-football player who turned to drug pushing. And there
would be no hint of a CIA involvement and no international
implications."

Gregory turned slightly away from Crumwell and sighed with
disbelief.

"You see, Mr. Gregory," Crumwell continued, "FBI Inspector
Anthony Miller became involved with foreign agents and was using
his position within the FBI for personal gain. *I'm actually* with the
Secret Service, working in conjunction with the FBI on this case. I

guess you're wondering then, why am I not in Washington, protecting the president of the United States. Well it's a long and complicated story."

"More lies, Crumwell?" Gregory said.

"Only the truth, Mr. Gregory. And if it were not for your good friend, Alvin Walker, everything would have been cleared up at the Airport. My men were about to put you in protective custody when Walker came along. Don't you think that if we wanted you dead, we could have killed you at the Airport?"

"Your men came very close to killing me while I was in a phone booth waiting to talk to my Uncle Max."

"I've heard about that incident," said Crumwell. "And you're lucky to be alive. But once again, the CIA hit squad was responsible. When we learned that you were heading for the Airport, we wanted to intercept you there and protect you from the CIA hit squad. I know this is all confusing for you, but you must understand that Inspector Miller was not in charge. While he was giving orders to have you murdered, *I* was actually in charge. We've had Miller under scrutiny for months. We didn't take Miller into custody before, because of the vital role which he played in this case."

"And what role was that, Crumwell?" Gregory asked.

"We want his 'superiors' badly," Crumwell said. "We want his 'contacts'. And in order to do that, we had to make it appear that he was still in control. We didn't want them to run for cover."

"How did you know I'd be at the Airport that night?"

"Through our sources, we learned that you had contacted your uncle, whose phone had been tapped for quite some time. We knew you'd be there."

"You have an answer for everything, don't you?"

"The worst is yet to come," said Crumwell. He tapped the car door window suddenly, trying to get the attention of the agent standing outside.

The agent opened the door and Crumwell said. "Let's go for a ride."

The two agents got into the car. One sat behind the wheel and the other sat on the passenger side.

Gregory was silent as the car pulled off slowly. He rolled down the window slightly so that he could get some fresh air.

"Okay, Crumwell." Gregory said. "How much worse can it get?"

"Before your Uncle Max retired as FBI Director last year, he learned that Inspector Anthony Miller was working with two high ranking members of the CIA, who also had some very strong connections within the Pentagon. Now, this CIA duo was selling classified information to the Soviet Union for very large sums of money. The type of information they were selling was high technology—the airborne laser guidance system, to name one, for example.

"Through the use of wiretapping and bugging devices, your Uncle Max eventually accumulated enough data to put away a lot of people, in very high places, for a very long time. But instead of doing his job to expose these people, your uncle decided to 'use' them and make a profit. He wanted a 'cut', a piece of the action."

"That's a lie," Gregory protested. "It's not true. My uncle was an honest man; a decent man."

"You're right, Gregory," Crumwell agreed. "He 'was' until he became weak with greed. He had planned to retire and the large sums of money exchanging hands looked very good to him. Your uncle always loved the good life. He wanted much more. He got in over his head. Things got out of control."

Gregory stared at Crumwell with disbelief.

"His adversaries," Crumwell continued, "started to put the pressure on him. And to save his own neck, he told the CIA duo that he was not working alone and that if anything were to happen to him, everyone involved with the selling of secrets to the Soviet Union would be exposed. And that's where you come in. Your uncle told them that he had sent the disk to you."

There was a moment of silence as the car approached a traffic light and came to a complete stop. Gregory leaned his head backward against the seat and closed his eyes thoughtfully. When the traffic light changed to green, the car pulled off.

"I know that all of this must be hard for you to take," Crumwell said, "but let me assure you, it is all true. You must understand the devastating impact of your uncle's position. He had in his hands the power to expose the illicit dealings of members of the FBI, the CIA and the KGB. Your uncle got in over his head and his plan failed.

"The Russians did not want the flow of U.S. Military secrets to suddenly stop, nor did they want their intelligence people here in the U.S. to be exposed. So initially, your uncle convinced everyone involved to take him in as a partner. But there was a problem, Mr. Gregory. 'You' became a loose end. Your uncle had told them that you *knew everything* and that you had the disk in a safe place. And that made everyone nervous. You became the new threat. And it was agreed that you had to be exterminated."

"To show good faith," Crumwell continued, "when the initial attempts to recover the disk from you failed, your uncle agreed to help them trap and kill you."

"That's a lie, Crumwell!" Gregory snapped. "My uncle would never do anything to hurt me"

Then Crumwell said, "How do you think the CIA hit squad found you so quickly at that phone booth, a few nights back? Your uncle told you he'd call you back and insisted that you wait right there. You had given him your exact location. He had just enough time to contact the hit squad. They would have tried again at the Airport if my men had not intercepted. Each time you talked to your uncle that night, we knew about it."

Gregory stared thoughtfully for a moment at Crumwell, and considered the possibility of there being some truth to what Crumwell had been telling him. But he found it very difficult to believe that his Uncle Max, the man who had been like a father to him all of those many years, could stoop so low as to help the CIA to murder his own blood—a member of his own family.

"Your uncle had no choice," Crumwell continued. "But then he realized that once his adversaries had 'you' out of the way, there would be nothing standing in the way of them killing *him*, as they had originally planned. So it was 'that' realization that prompted him to leave a tape recorded message for you on his telephone answering machine, informing you to use the disk to your advantage."

Gregory looked at Crumwell suddenly with an expression of surprise on his face, as if to ask: "How did he know that?"

"Yes," said Crumwell. "We knew about the recorded message, too."

It was all a trick, Gregory told himself. The FBI would say or do anything to obtain that valuable disk. But Gregory believed that as long as they "thought" he had the disk, he was still in the ball-game.

"The disk is a matter of National Security, Mr. Gregory," Crumwell said firmly. "The disk would supply us with names, dates and locations. The impact of this information could lead even to the White House. Through your uncle's intelligence work, he also uncovered a plot to assassinate the President of the United States. So *now* you know why the Secret Service is involved."

There was a pause.

"Okay," said Gregory abruptly, "so I do have access to the disk."

"Where?" asked Crumwell.

"One thing at a time," said Gregory. "You told me that my wife is alive."

"It's true," Mr. Gregory. "She's alive and well."

"Take me to her," Gregory demanded. "Take me to her now. And then, I hand over the disk to you."

"We're on our way to join her now," said Crumwell.

There was a pause.

Gregory looked thoughtfully at Crumwell for a moment, and then he stared straight ahead as the car travelled at a modest rate of speed along the well-lighted street.

~~~~

Within only a few moments they arrived at Slater Memorial Hospital. The two agents in the front seat of the car exited first. Gregory followed Crumwell as the other two FBI agents tagged closely behind Gregory. When they reached the lobby of the hospital, the two agents stopped suddenly as if to guard the entrance of the hospital, as Gregory and Crumwell continued toward the elevator.

Gregory stood slightly behind Crumwell, off to his left, as they waited for the elevator doors to open. The doors opened and two people got off—an elderly man and his daughter. Then Gregory

and Crumwell entered the elevator and the doors closed. They were
alone. Crumwell pressed the button for the sixth floor.

Gregory was leaning against the wall of the elevator as
Crumwell stood at his left eyeing him.

"Did my men do that?" Crumwell asked.

"What?" said Gregory.

"The cut on your forehead, there."

"No," Gregory said dryly. He paused, and then said,
"Hilderbrant. It was Hilderbrant."

"You should let a doctor take a look at that," Crumwell urged.

"I'm fine," Gregory insisted.

"It's a nasty cut."

"No. I'm fine."

At the sixth floor, the elevator stopped. Crumwell allowed
Gregory to get off first and he followed. Standing at the nurses'
station were two FBI agents. To the right of the main desk, all of
the rooms down the lengthy hallway were empty except two. The
FBI had that specific portion of the floor sealed off.

Gregory was walking slightly behind Crumwell as they moved
at a moderate pace down the hall, which, with the exception of an
FBI agent standing guard just outside Room 607, was deserted. It
was that room to which Crumwell lead Gregory. He opened the
door and stepped to the side, allowing Gregory to enter first. When
Gregory entered the room, his eyes lit up with joy. To his surprise,
lying in the bed was his beautiful wife, Freda. She was indeed alive
and well. He called her name and she responded by trying to sit
upright in bed. The white bandage was still wrapped completely
around her head and the bandage which covered the cut on her
neck was also in place.

Gregory rushed over to the bed and embraced his wife.

"Oh, Steven," she said, holding him tightly. "I thought I'd never see you again." She was sobbing. "I thought you were dead."

"Oh, Freda," Gregory said, "thank God you're okay."

"Just hold me; don't let me go."

"I've missed you so much," Gregory said with his eyes closed, as he continued to embrace his wife tightly. There was a brief pause, and then Gregory held her at arm's length. "Let me look at you. Are you okay? Did they hurt you?"

"No," Freda answered. "But who are those people? They wouldn't tell me anything. I asked for you day after day, but they wouldn't tell me anything."

Gregory looked toward the door and noticed that he and his wife were alone in the hospital room. Crumwell had moved from the doorway and had left the room completely to allow Gregory a moment of privacy with his wife.

"They're Federal agents, honey. FBI." Gregory said.

"Yes," said Freda, "they told me that, but I didn't believe them. The FBI doesn't hold people hostage in a hospital. What's going on, Steven. Why are these people doing this?"

"It's a long story, honey," said Gregory.

"Then tell me, Steven. I want to leave this place. I don't want to spend another minute here. I don't like it here. They kept me drugged most of the time so that I wouldn't try to escape again. I tried once, but I failed. And when I told them that I wanted to see you, they told me that they couldn't find you, and that they were trying to locate you so that they could protect you. But protect you from what? They would never tell me."

"Like I said, honey," said Gregory, "it's a long story."

"I don't care how long the explanation is. I want you to tell me. I have the right to know. I've been worried sick about you for the last few days. I thought I'd never see you again. I thought you were dead and that these goons were lying to me."

They embraced once again and there was a moment of silence as Gregory's wife sobbed on his shoulder.

"It's okay, baby," Gregory said. "We're going to be okay. And yes, you do have the right to know what's going on and I'm going to tell you. It has something to do with my Uncle Max." Gregory sighed, and then continued. "He learned too much about a corrupt system."

~~~~

Standing just outside the room was special agent Crumwell. For nearly ten minutes he stood there, allowing Gregory some time with his wife. Then suddenly, in the distance, Crumwell saw FBI Agent Tucker moving quickly down the hall toward him. Crumwell moved slightly away from the door and met Tucker.

"What have you got," asked Crumwell.

"Not much good news, I'm afraid," said Tucker. "There has been no word on Hilderbrant, yet. I have some men combing Gregory's neighborhood now. Hilderbrant will turn up sooner or later. Preferably dead."

"Any luck with the disk?" Crumwell asked.

"No trace of the disk, yet," said Tucker.

"Continue the search," Crumwell instructed firmly.

~~~~

"So what's going to happen to us now?" Gregory's wife asked him as he sat on the edge of her hospital bed.

"We're going to be just fine, honey," Gregory answered. "I won't let them hurt you. It's all over, now. You don't have to worry about anything."

The door opened suddenly and Crumwell entered the room. "We have to talk, now, Mr. Gregory," he said.

Gregory looked at his wife and gave her a kiss on the lips. As he attempted to get up from the bed, his wife pulled him close and they embraced.

"Don't leave me," she whispered in his ear.

"It's okay, honey," he said. "I'm going to be right outside the door. We're just going to talk. That's all."

Gregory stood up and joined Crumwell at the door. As he left the room, he looked back at his wife. And he continued to look at her until Crumwell closed the door.

"C'mon," said Crumwell, "let's take a walk."

The two men started slowly down the lengthy hall, opposite the nurses' station.

"Where are we going?" asked Gregory.

"There's a visitor's lounge ahead. We can go there and talk."

As they passed the third room down from his wife's room, Gregory heard someone call his name. He stopped suddenly because the voice sounded familiar. It was the voice of a man whom he thought he'd never hear again. The man, as he rested there in the hospital bed, had heard Gregory's voice as Gregory and Crumwell walked past the door which had been left open.

Gregory entered the room slowly and lying in the bed was a man with a large bandage on the right side of his chest and right shoulder. The man was lying on his back and was operating the electric bed controls, slowly raising his back so that he could sit up in bed. The man in the bed was Alvin Walker.

"Steven," said Alvin, his face reflecting the pain from his chest and shoulder wound.

"Alvin," said Gregory, reaching for his friend's hand. "You sonofabitch—you're okay!" Gregory was smiling.

"I thought I'd never see you again, pal," said Alvin.

"Gee!" said Gregory, "I thought you were dead meat when I left you there in the woods."

"All I can remember is getting shot and you helping me get out of the car. When I woke up, I was here in the hospital, all patched up."

"Thank God you're okay, pal."

"Thank God for you too, pal," said Alvin.

Remembering that Crumwell was standing in the doorway, Gregory said "Look, don't try to talk anymore. You get some rest. I'll look in on you later. I've got to go now."

Alvin glanced at Crumwell standing at the door, and then he looked back at Gregory and said. "Be careful, Steven. Take care."

Gregory nodded his head as he looked at Alvin, and then he left the room.

Without speaking another word, Gregory and Crumwell walked down the hall to the lounge area. Gregory thought of his wife. He was thankful that she was still alive. And there was his good friend Alvin, who had survived the gunshot wound. But how long would either of them live after that night?

Gregory found it difficult to trust Crumwell after being misled for such a long time by Hilderbrant. They were both in the same business of doing anything to get what they wanted, even if it did mean lying and twisting the truth to hurt other people. Gregory just couldn't believe that his Uncle Max would set him up to be murdered as Crumwell had suggested earlier.

But Gregory would now have to play his last card. He felt certain that as long as Crumwell thought that Gregory knew the location of the disk, Gregory would be safe.

Agent Tucker was leaning backward against the wall, with his arms folded, when Gregory and Crumwell reached the lounge area. He directed Gregory to a green sofa with a gesture of his hand.

Gregory sat on the sofa and leaned forward with a sigh.

Crumwell sat beside Gregory on the sofa. "Okay, Mr. Gregory," he said, the time has come. I'd like for you to tell me the location of the disk."

Gregory was silent for a moment. He looked at Crumwell, and then shifted his gaze to Tucker, then back to Crumwell. "Okay," he said finally. "I'll tell you. The disk could be just about anywhere now."

"Please. No games, Mr. Gregory," Crumwell said.

Once again there was a pause, and then Gregory said, "Look, when I heard your men breaking into my home, I panicked. I had found the map—the instructions for how to locate the disk—wrapped in plastic in the bottle of wine that my Uncle Max had sent to me. Well, what I did was think about it for a moment. *At that time*, I was sure that my wife was dead and that I was about to die. All I could think of at that point was to do all I could to hurt the FBI—since I would soon be dead within a couple of minutes"

Crumwell looked at Tucker, then back at Gregory.

"So, as I stood there in the bathroom alone," Gregory continued. "I thought of how important that disk must be to the FBI—considering the fact that so many people wanted to get their hands on it. So, without viewing the instructions, I ripped up the map that was attached to the cork—the wine stopper thing—and I tossed it into the toilet bowl and gave it a flush."

Crumwell and Tucker stared speechlessly at Gregory for a moment. Crumwell lowered his head and sighed with disappointment.

"And now that I'm no longer important to you, what's going to happen to me and my wife?" Gregory asked.

"It's going to be a terrible setback for us," said Crumwell, as he rose from the sofa, "but unfortunately, as long as the CIA hit squad knows that you are alive, your wife and family will be in danger because many people believe that you have *knowledge of the contents* of the disk."

Gregory was silent for a moment, glancing at Crumwell and then Tucker.

"We're going to relocate you and your wife." Crumwell said to Gregory.

"You will both be given a new identity—home, birth records—the works. It will take a while to get used to it—the new identity and all—but it's better than taking chances on your own against the CIA hit squad."

Gregory was staring at Crumwell. He suddenly realized that Crumwell was on the level. What Crumwell had told him earlier in the car had all been true. Gregory admitted to himself that he really was leaning toward believing Crumwell's story initially, but he would also have to accept the possibility that his Uncle Max had given aid to the CIA hit squad to murder him. And that was the most difficult part to accept.

But no! Wait a moment, Gregory thought. If the FBI was able to wiretap his uncle's phone, then what was the CIA able to do? Two very powerful entities. The CIA could have intercepted and or collected the same info that the FBI had collected, Gregory determined. The CIA could have obtained Gregory's exact location at that phone booth without his uncle's assistance. Which means, Gregory concluded, his uncle Max had nothing to do with setting him up to be murdered by that CIA hit squad.

As Crumwell started to leave the lounge area, Gregory got to his feet and called, "Crumwell!"

Crumwell stopped and faced Gregory.

Gregory hesitated then said to the special agent, "I can't lie to you. I was testing you. I 'did' flush the notes—the information on the paper down the toilet, but *not until after I had read it*."

Crumwell moved back toward Gregory with renewed interest. "Then where, Gregory? Where is the disk?"

"If the map is correct," Gregory said, "the disk is in the back of the picture frame that hangs on the wall in my downtown office. It's an eleven by fourteen photo of my Uncle Max and me. A fishing trip photo of the two of us posing with fish that we caught. He sent it to me nearly a year ago."

Crumwell looked at Tucker suddenly and said, "Tucker get on it."

"Right," said Tucker.

~~~~

At 10:45 PM, six FBI agents forcibly entered Gregory's downtown office, kicking the door open. Agent Tucker moved promptly to the fishing trip picture of Gregory and his Uncle Max and removed it from the wall. With the picture frame in hand, he moved to an adjacent desk and placed the picture frame, face down, atop the desk. With a knife, he carefully cut and removed the cover from the back of the frame. And there it was. The disk that so many had died for. He paused momentarily then raised the disk close to his face and just stared at it with a nod of his head. Thumbs up!

~ ~ ~ ~

At the hospital, Crumwell was suddenly approached by an agent who revealed to him that they had found the disk in Gregory's office. With a loud victory yell, he said "Yeah!" He then walked down the hall toward Gregory.

"Thanks for your corporation, Mr. Gregory," said Crumwell. "You did the right thing. We have the disk."

"Yeah," Gregory said dryly.

"And I'm very sorry about your uncle. There is no credible evidence that he's still alive. Your uncle took a gamble and he lost. Even though his intentions initially were unethical, *some good did* 'ultimately', come out of this. Through your uncle's intelligence work, we will be able to expose and put away a lot of people—traitors— for a long time. And thanks to *your cooperation*, we can now make our move. You've done a great service to your country, Mr. Gregory. And I thank you."

There was a pause.

Then Crumwell left, leaving Gregory standing alone.

For a moment, Gregory stood there staring straight ahead, down that lengthy hall, thinking about what was to come—the relocation and a new life with his wife. And as he remembered his uncle, he was trying to forget.

~ ~ ~ ~

February 8.

He laid quietly alone in bed in a cheap motel room, recovering from a gunshot wound to the left side of his chest near his shoulder. He was lucky to be alive after losing so much blood.

A small Sony television set was on a stand in front of him near the foot of the bed. The CBS evening news with Dan Rather had just come on the tube.

"Good evening. Dan Rather reporting. Today, two high ranking CIA officials were taken into custody by the FBI for allegedly selling U.S. military secrets to the Soviet Union. CBS News has learned that the FBI has in its possession a compact disk, which contains information gathered by the former director of the FBI, Maxwell Craven, which reveal not only conversations between the two CIA officials and foreign agents, but also reveals a plot to assassinate the president of the United States.

"As we reported earlier in the week, the former FBI director disappeared recently without a trace. Authorities suspect foul play and fear he is already dead. Some sources tell us that the disk which the FBI now has in its possession reveal a multimillion dollar scheme which involved cooperation within the Pentagon, the CIA and even the FBI itself. For more, now, on the story, we have three reports from Washington. First—"

As he laid in bed staring at the television screen and listened to the news report, Carl Hilderbrant touched his bandaged wound gently.

About the Author

Lee Moore is a former LAPD, civilian, Martial Arts Instructor for The Los Angeles Police Department's Jeopardy Program, which is a gang prevention and intervention program. He is also a former employee at BofA's Los Angeles Data Center's Micrographics Department.